WAVES OF GRACE

ALSO BY BARBARA HINSKE

Available at Amazon in Print, Audio, and for Kindle

The Rosemont Series

Coming to Rosemont

Weaving the Strands

Uncovering Secrets

Drawing Close

Bringing Them Home

Shelving Doubts

Restoring What Was Lost

No Matter How Far

When Dreams There Be

Waves of Grace

Novellas

The Night Train

The Christmas Club (adapted for The Hallmark Channel, 2019)

Paws & Pastries

Sweets & Treats

Snowflakes, Cupcakes & Kittens

Workout Wishes & Valentine Kisses

Wishes of Home

Wishful Tails

Back in the Pack

Novels in the Guiding Emily Series

Guiding Emily (adapted for The Hallmark Channel, 2023)

The Unexpected Path

Over Every Hurdle

Down the Aisle

From the Heart

Novels in the "Who's There?!" Collection

Deadly Parcel

Final Circuit

CONNECT WITH BARBARA HINSKE ONLINE

Sign up for her newsletter at **BarbaraHinske.com**
    Goodreads.com/BarbaraHinske
    Facebook.com/BHinske
    Instagram/barbarahinskeauthor
    TikTok.com/BarbaraHinske
    Pinterest.com/BarbaraHinske
    X.com/BarbaraHinske
    Search for **Barbara Hinske on YouTube**
    bhinske@gmail.com

WAVES OF GRACE
THE TENTH NOVEL IN THE ROSEMONT SERIES

BARBARA HINSKE

Waves of Grace
by Barbara Hinske

This book may not be reproduced in whole or in part without written permission of the author, with the exception of brief quotations within book reviews or articles. This book is a work of fiction. Any resemblance to actual persons, living or dead, or places or events is coincidental.

Copyright @ 2024 Barbara Hinske

All rights reserved.

ISBN: 9798991115100

LCCN: 2024914163

Casa del Northern Publishing

Phoenix, Arizona

No AI Training: Without in any way limiting the author's and publisher's exclusive rights under copyright, any use of this publication to "train" generative artificial intelligence (AI) technologies to generate text is expressly prohibited. The author reserves all rights to license uses of this work for generative AI training and development of machine learning language models.

In loving memory of my mother and grandmother. These remarkable women taught me to sew and, more importantly, how to live a worthwhile life.

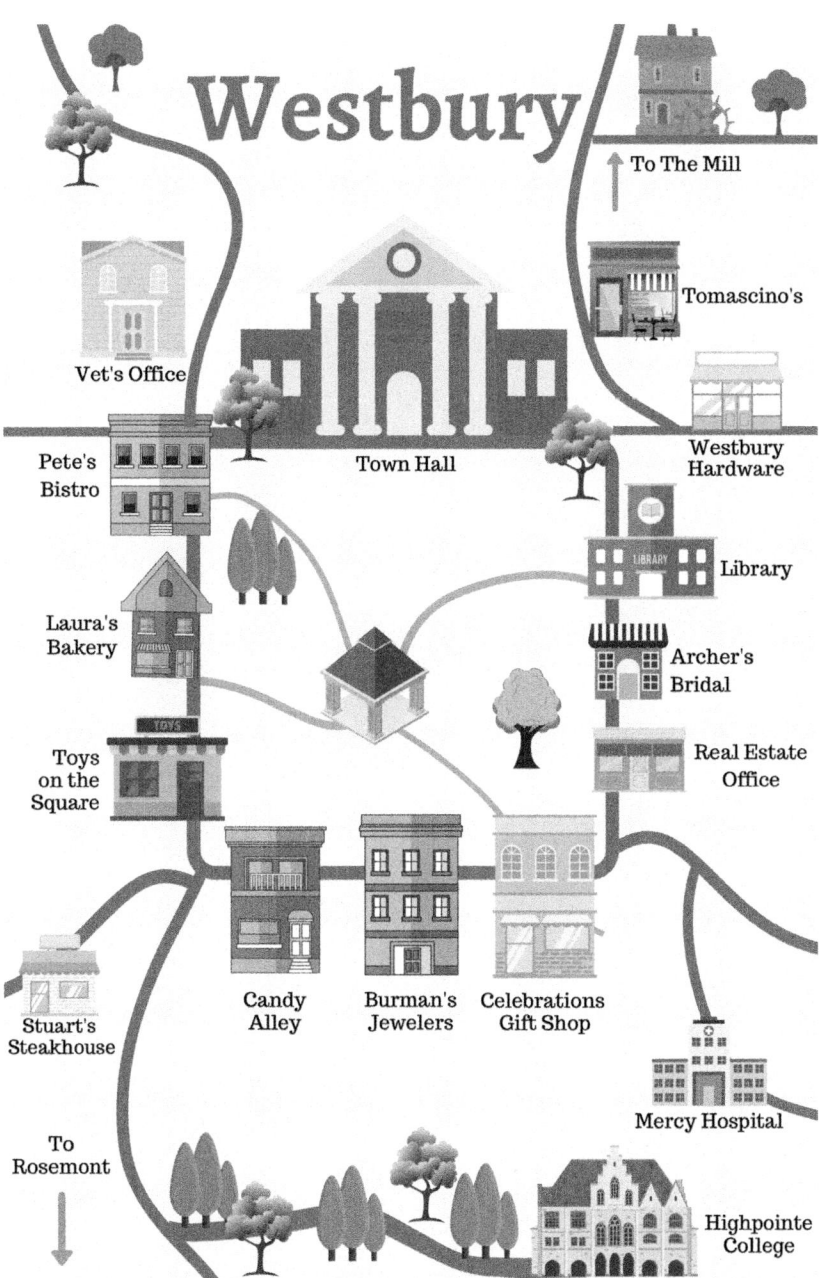

PROLOGUE

Alistair—almost three years earlier:

It was time. I'd been hiding long enough. Tonight was the perfect opportunity. Simply put, I was tired of being alone.

The old, glass doorknob rattled as the cantankerous latch gave free, and the door opened on its rusty hinges. I flattened myself against the wall behind the now-open attic door. When I'd been alive, my six-foot-five, two-hundred-ten-pound frame would not have fit in the slim space. Now—it would be no problem.

John Allen took the creaky steps up to the attic two at a time.

Maggie Martin rested her foot on the bottom step. "The inflatable goblin should be in its box on the far side of the attic, under the window," she called after him. This was the nice woman with whom I'd spent the night in the attic shortly after she'd moved into Rosemont. I'd made it seem like the wind had blown the door shut. I'd only wanted her to while away a bit of time with me in the attic. She'd sounded so nice when I'd heard her talking to the little dog I helped bring into her life.

I'd even managed to arrange our collection of vintage silver in one of the discarded cabinets. The best part of every Saturday during my adult life, when I'd been Rosemont's butler, had been spent polishing the stuff. I wanted her to see it. How was I supposed to know that the lock would stick, and she'd be stranded in the cold, drafty attic overnight? I'd helped her open the window, which had allowed her to summon help. The whole debacle had thrown me for a loop, and I'd been sulking in the attic ever since—but not for much longer. Tonight was the night. Maggie and John were going to learn that Rosemont had another permanent resident—one who had lived here far longer than they had. They needed to know that Rosemont had a ghost in residence, and I wanted them to understand that I was friendly, responsible, and helpful. Just as I had been during my life.

"Got it," John said as he approached the steps.

"Good. I'll pour the candy into our big, orange bowl while you get him set up and plugged in."

They exited the attic, and I slipped out after them. I floated down the stairs until we reached the first floor. I hadn't been in the living room in decades. The upholstered furniture was new, but I recognized every side table and the prominent stone fireplace.

Two dogs lay next to each other on the hearthrug. The

small terrier mix rose to a sitting position and stared at me, her ears erect and the hair standing up on the back of her neck. The golden retriever lifted his head, opened one eye, and then thumped his tail on the carpet in a gesture of recognition and approval. Dogs are intuitive creatures. The terrier looked at her companion, then settled back on her haunches and put her chin on her paws. We were going to get along just fine.

My gaze shifted to the painting above the hearth. I knew they'd taken down the Thomas Cole masterpiece that had hung there in my day because it had been stored in the attic. I was prepared to dislike its replacement but found the painting of a woman and children picking blackberries in the sunshine quite pleasing. This couple had a refined eye for art. I approved.

To my right, Maggie poured the smallest Hershey's chocolate bars I'd ever seen into a bowl. They'd been my favorite candy. I crossed to the bowl as Maggie flipped a switch to turn on the entryway light and stepped out the front door.

"Where do you want him?" John asked.

"I think we should put him on the other side of the door," Maggie said. "He'll be in the way of the trick-or-treaters if we leave him where he is."

"I'll move him," John replied. "Just tell me when you're satisfied."

I watched, dumbstruck, as John wrestled the goblin into a new position. It dipped and bobbed, narrowly missing the pavement. That thing was almost as flexible as I was.

Maggie tilted her head to one side. "I'm not sure. Maybe we should put him back where he was."

John sighed and bent to pick up the contraption. A thought popped into my head. I returned to the bowl of candy sitting on the large, round table in the foyer. Maggie had just filled it to the brim. Acting as quickly as I could, I levitated a candy bar and steered it into the pot of a large, white orchid that sat in the center of the table. This first piece was followed by another, and then another, until half of the candy bars had been relocated and the bowl was noticeably less full.

I pressed myself into the shadows as Maggie and John came back inside.

"It's almost dark," John said. "We should have trick-or-treaters any time now."

"We're all set, and I've got …" She stopped in mid-sentence, pointing at the bowl. "This was full when I went outside."

John looked at the bowl. "You're sure?"

"Positive."

I moved closer, giddy with anticipation. "Look in the orchid's pot!" I wanted to shout.

Maggie and John turned in unison toward the hearth. "Roman!" John said in a voice so serious and stern it made me jump back. "BAD DOG!"

Roman lifted his head, looking justifiably confused.

John crouched next to the big dog. "You know better than to get food off of the counters. What's gotten into you?"

"Are you sure it's his fault?" Maggie asked. "It'd be so unlike him."

"Who else could it be? Eve isn't tall enough." John grasped Roman by the collar and, in the practiced motions of an experienced veterinarian, examined Roman's mouth and took a whiff of his breath. "There are no signs of any wrapper scraps in his mouth, and he doesn't smell like chocolate. This is so odd."

"Isn't chocolate harmful to dogs? Do you need to pump his stomach?"

"It is, but I don't think that'll be necessary. I'll keep an eye on him. He'll probably throw up the whole lot in a little while. I'm going to put both of these guys on the back patio, so we won't have a mess to clean up in the house."

"Good idea. I can see the first group of kids coming up the driveway."

"I'll be right back. Are you done with the pizza? There's another slice left—and it's got your name on it."

"Just leave it in the box on the counter. I'll get it when there's a lull in the action."

"Right," John said. He whistled for the dogs to follow him. I trailed along. I had never intended to get Roman into trouble. Just like when I'd caused the attic door to blow shut on Maggie, another of my schemes had gone awry.

John opened the kitchen door and signaled for the dogs to go outside. "It's a nice evening—you'll enjoy yourselves." He bent and rubbed between Roman's ears. "I'll be back to check on you, boy. You shouldn't have done that, but I'll take good care of you."

John shut the door and turned on the patio lights before hurrying to rejoin Maggie.

I needed to make things right with Roman and Eve. Starting off my downstairs time with them on the wrong foot was not my plan. I was circling the kitchen island when my eyes fell on a large, square cardboard box. I lifted the lid and took a whiff. It smelled like tomatoes and cheese. Was this that thing called pizza that John had been referring to?

Dogs had loved table scraps in my day and I felt certain they still did. I levitated the remaining triangular piece and was quite proud of myself when I passed through the patio door, the pizza coming with me unscathed.

Roman and Eve got to their feet and came toward me, mouths open and tails wagging. I tore the slice into two uneven pieces, giving the larger one to Roman. He ate it in one gulp, licked his lips appreciatively, and nodded to me. I was forgiven for the candy bar incident—I was sure of it.

Satisfied that I'd done something right, I headed for the front door. We hadn't celebrated Halloween in my time, but I found the high spirits of the children quite engaging. The only improvement I would make would be to the ridiculously unrealistic ghost costumes. I certainly didn't spend my days in a sloppy, dirty sheet—and I'd never seen any ghost with an oversized, gaping, menacing mouth. The older children were inclined to these macabre renditions. I was going to have nightmares about them for weeks.

A large group of kids moved away from the door. The next bunch had just started up the long driveway leading to Rosemont.

"I'm going to check on Roman," John said.

"Will you bring me that last slice of pizza?"

I bobbed in excitement. Surely they'd figure out I was here from the empty box.

"I'm still hungry," Maggie said, "and I don't want to eat candy."

"Will do."

Maggie smiled as the children climbed the wide, stone steps to the massive front door. Six children cried, "Trick or treat!"

I floated into the space that John had occupied in order to get a closer look at their costumes.

Maggie held out the candy bowl and five of the children grabbed one piece each. The sixth child, in an elaborate pirate costume, took a handful.

One of the adult men accompanying them stepped forward and told the boy that he could only take one.

The boy tightened his grip. "I'm a pirate!"

"That's okay," Maggie began, reaching into the bowl to give additional candy to the other children in the group.

The man shook his head. "My son has to obey the rules." He addressed the boy. "You're dressed like a pirate, but that doesn't mean you can act like one."

Maggie stepped back.

I watched the other children as they waited patiently for their friend to do as he was told. I was admiring the caped red-and-blue costume with a large yellow "S" on the chest worn by one boy when I noticed his shoelaces were untied. That spelled trouble. I wasn't sure I could remember how to tie a shoe, but I gave it my best shot. I had it securely knotted by the time the recalcitrant child had come around and returned his ill-gotten booty to the candy bowl.

The group was hurrying away from the door when John returned from the kitchen.

Maggie glanced up at him. "What's wrong? Is Roman all right?"

"He's fine," John said.

Maggie nodded. "Good." She pushed the candy bowl into his hands. "I'll just go get that last slice of pizza."

"That's just it." John furrowed his brow. "The box was empty."

They looked at each other.

"That last slice was in the box when I put the dogs outside."

"Neither of us left the front door until you did—just now."

"I know. It's so weird," John said.

"TRICK OR TREAT!" yelled the next group of children.

Maggie and John turned back to the door.

By the time the last piece of candy had been given out and John had turned out the porch light, I was pooped. And a bit perplexed because they still hadn't figured out I was here.

"I've got to turn in," John said. "I'm scheduled for an early surgery in the morning."

"I'm tired, too."

"I'll bring the dogs in," John said. "Why don't you go upstairs and start getting ready for bed? You take longer than I do."

Maggie leaned in and gave John a kiss. "You're the best."

She climbed the stairs to the second floor, and I went with her.

John was correct—Maggie spent a lot of time smearing lotions onto her face and then wiping them off before washing it and smearing more lotion onto her face. The whole thing seemed pointless to me—she looked the same both before and after. When she started on another involved process with her teeth, I decided to explore the bedroom.

The curtains that hung at the tall windows were new, but the view would be as I remembered it. The bed was placed as it always had been. I was scrutinizing the fireplace—remembering the fires that had burned there every evening from September through mid-May—when something glinted at me from below in the bin that held kindling.

I moved closer. A pair of dark-rimmed spectacles caught the shaft of light from the bathroom. The shape of the frame made me think they were of recent vintage. By the size of them, I'd guess they were John's. I had just maneuvered them into place next to a man's wallet on the nightstand I presumed was his when John came into the room, trailed by the two dogs.

They both gave me a short wag of their tails as they headed for their baskets on either side of the bed.

John attached a thin, rectangular box with a glass screen to a long wire before placing it on his nightstand. He turned as Maggie switched off the bathroom light and moved to her side of the bed. "Where in the world did you find my reading glasses?" he asked, picking them up and gesturing to her with them.

Maggie's eyes grew wide. "I … I didn't find them. I haven't seen them in weeks."

John lowered his hand. "Are you playing a Halloween joke on me?"

Maggie shook her head slowly. "I wish I were."

John pursed his lips. "When I was a kid, there were stories about Rosemont being haunted. I didn't believe them at the time …"

"And now?"

John shrugged.

Maggie turned back the duvet. "I think those rumors may have been right. At least he seems helpful. Maybe he's a friendly ghost."

I hovered at the foot of the bed. We were making progress.

"What do you remember about this ghost of Rosemont?"

They got into bed and Maggie nestled next to John. He put his arm around her and drew her close. "Not much. His name was Alistair, and he had been the butler here for over fifty years." They fell silent. Soon, the only sound was the quiet snoring of the two dogs.

My work was cut out for me—I needed to show them how lovely it would be to live with Alistair—the decidedly friendly ghost. I retraced my steps down the hall and took myself into the attic. Even a ghost needs his beauty sleep. In fact, sometimes I slept for years.

CHAPTER 1

Maggie Martin walked to the guardrail of the scenic viewpoint where she and John Allen had pulled off the highway. The sun rode high in a cloudless, azure sky. Trees dressed in leaves ranging from pale gold to deepest crimson fanned out in front of them, like graduated samples in a paint deck. She corralled her shoulder-length, chestnut bob with her hands as the stiff breeze tried to force it into her face.

"This is magnificent," she said to John, without taking her eyes from the spectacular scene that ran to the horizon. "Fall in Westbury is beautiful, but it doesn't hold a candle to Vermont. I can see why people travel here to leaf peep. I'm glad you insisted we come."

John didn't respond.

Maggie tore her eyes from the view to turn to him.

John stood on the driver's side of their rental car, his

hand shading his eyes as he stared into the distance in the other direction.

"It's gorgeous no matter which way you turn," she said, crunching across the gravel to join him.

He pointed to the tree line along the horizon. "Do you see that?"

Maggie looked to where he was pointing. "I see more of the most magnificent fall foliage I've ever seen. If I didn't know better, I'd say I'm looking at a photo that's been color enhanced."

"Take a closer look," he said. "Where the farthest tree line meets the sky."

Maggie followed his lead and shielded her eyes. "There's a whitish haze about the trees. I can't see it very well. Could it be clouds?"

John shook his head slowly. "I don't think so."

"What, then?" Maggie sucked in her breath. "OMG—do you think that's a wildfire?"

"I'm afraid so."

Maggie flung open the back passenger door and dug around in a duffel bag, pulling out a pair of binoculars. "Here," she said, thrusting them at her husband. "Now you can quit teasing me about packing them."

John trained the binoculars on the horizon, moving them slowly from left to right.

Maggie stood at his shoulder, biting her lip. "Well?"

John handed her the binoculars. "It's a forest fire, all right. See for yourself."

Maggie quickly confirmed his conclusion. "All I see is

smoke. I don't see anything orange, but the smoke is getting darker on the eastern edge." She lowered the binoculars and faced John. "Should we call someone?"

John nodded and pulled his phone out of his pocket. "That's a pretty good-sized fire. I'm sure they already know about it, but it doesn't hurt to call it in."

Maggie listened to his side of his brief conversation with the 911 operator. "They're aware of it," she stated.

John nodded. "First reports came in shortly before noon. The wind has spread it rapidly. They have fire crews on the scene."

"That's good. They'll put it out."

"Hopefully," John said. He pointed to the trees crowding the road on the other side of the highway. "They got near record rainfall this year and the undergrowth is dense. The dispatcher said that they've been worried about fire danger."

"Does Vermont have a wildfire season?"

"I don't think so," John replied. "The dispatcher said it's too early to tell, but they think this one was man-made."

"Arson?"

"Or someone careless with a campfire." John took the binoculars back from her. "The smoke along the tree line is now dark gray," he said.

"Does that mean it's getting closer? Are we in danger here?"

"I'm sure it's still a long way away, but we're not familiar with this area. I'd like to head back to our hotel."

"By all means," Maggie said, opening the front passenger door and sliding into her seat. "The last thing we need is to become idiot tourists who have to be rescued because we weren't smart enough to turn around."

"I'm glad you agree," John said, slipping behind the wheel and starting the engine. "Let's get back to The Wishing Tree Inn to find out what's going on. We'll probably learn that everything has been contained and we can continue leaf peeping."

JOHN PULLED into the lot of The Wishing Tree Inn at three-thirty. They made their way around the charming, red brick building and headed for the steps leading to the wide expanse of porch.

"Am I imagining things, or can you smell smoke?" John asked.

"I was wondering the same thing," Maggie sniffed the air. She gestured toward the town square across from the inn. A mature linden tree stood in the square, its generous limbs festooned with scraps of paper tied to the lowest branches with ribbons that bounced in the stiff breeze. "I hope the fire doesn't destroy the town's namesake. People around here actually believe that wishes hung on that tree really do come true. Look at all of them!"

"I think the town—and that tree—will be safe." He pointed to a fire hydrant at the curb. "It looks like the municipal water supply protects this area."

"Good. That means we'll be safe at the inn, too."

They began climbing the steps to the porch when the

front door to the inn opened and a middle-aged man rushed out, letting the door shut with a thwack right in front of Maggie and John.

"Oh … sorry," the man said, rushing back to open the door for them.

"No worries," John said. "It looks like you're in a hurry."

The man nodded. "There's a wildfire outside of town. It's threatening an animal shelter and we're looking for volunteers to help settle the animals into our brand new shelter. It's not even open yet, but we got volunteers to come in this afternoon to finish construction. We now need people to bring blankets and food for the evacuees—and medical supplies."

John's head snapped up.

"We've picked up a lot of strays who ran away from home and suffered injuries in the fire, too."

A pickup truck pulled in front of the inn and honked the horn.

"I've gotta go. We stopped here for a load of supplies." He pointed to the plastic crates piled high in the truck bed. "We knew the inn would have extra blankets and towels." His voice trailed off as he ran to the waiting truck.

John looked at Maggie. "They'll need medical help."

She nodded.

"Do you mind if I check with my buddy, Stan? Maybe I can stop by his veterinary clinic to grab supplies and take them to this new shelter."

"Of course not—but I'm coming with you," Maggie replied.

John reached for the phone in his pocket to place the call to his long-time friend from veterinary school when it began to ring.

"Speak of the devil," John said. "I was just going to call you."

For the second time that day, Maggie listened to John's side of a conversation.

"I'm not surprised that your waiting room is wall-to-wall with walk-ins bringing in pets injured during their evacuation. I'm not licensed in Vermont, but is there anything I can do to help?"

John silently nodded his head while he listened to the other vet. "I understand you can't leave your practice to go to the shelter until you've seen everyone at your clinic. I wouldn't abandon my clinic, either." He drew a deep breath. "I was just about to call you to see if you have extra first aid supplies that I—Maggie and I—could drive to the shelter."

John did more listening. "That's a great idea. Put me on your books as a veterinarian technician. I can treat animals—under your supervision."

Maggie touched John's elbow and pulled him with her toward their car.

"We'll be at your place in ten minutes to pick up those supplies. I'll treat the injured animals. Maggie and I will stay at the shelter until they're all taken care of."

John quickened his pace. "I'll text you to let you know how things are at the shelter. Maybe it won't be as bad as you fear and you won't have to go there after you're finished at your clinic." He tapped at his phone to end the call.

They reached their car.

"It's bad," John said as he unlocked their car. "Stan said he's seeing very serious injuries—burns, lacerations, respiratory distress."

"Those poor animals," Maggie said. "I keep thinking of Roman and Eve and Blossom, Bubbles, and Buttercup. How terrified they'd be."

They both got into the car.

John started the engine and swiveled to face her. "I may be there all night, sweetheart. Are you sure you want to come with me? If it gets to be too much for you, you can always drive back here to the inn."

"Too much for me?" Maggie asked with a large dose of indignation. "I can't provide medical care, but I can comfort the animals, help with feeding, cleanup, and logistics, and support you. I'm going to be by your side every step of the way." Her tone was firm. "Let's get going. It sounds like we have no time to lose."

John squeezed her hand, and they were on their way.

CHAPTER 2

Pam Olson helped unload the last dog from the large cargo van at the entrance to Fur Friends Sanctuary. The fifteen evacuees from the neighboring town's shelter had been safely deposited into crates and cages that the volunteers had completed assembling not more than thirty minutes earlier. In front of her, in the reception area, all six stray dogs the driver had picked up on the way over had burn injuries.

"The two veterinarians in Linden Falls are swamped with walk-ins from people fleeing the burn areas with their injured pets," an intake staffer told Pam. "One of them has sent a senior vet tech, but that's all the help we're going to get until their practices close for the day."

They both looked at a German shepherd whimpering pitifully as he pawed at his badly burned ears.

"We'll have to do the best we can," the staff member said.

Pam's eyes pooled with tears as she looked at the array of miserable animals in front of her. "This is just the first wave," she said. "I don't know how to help them."

"No worries." A confident voice sounded behind her.

Pam turned to see a man she had met on Saturday while working at her mother's farmers market booth. He was the veterinarian in town on vacation with his wife, the pretty woman who had bought stacks of fall table linens from Pam's mother. They'd also purchased several of the dog collars her mother sold to benefit the shelter—and he'd made a generous donation, too. And now he was addressing her, his wife at his side.

"I graduated from veterinary school with one of your local vets," John said. "We're visiting him and his wife. Anyway, he just asked me to jump in here until he can get away. I'm officially here as a vet tech."

Pam almost collapsed against him in relief.

Maggie put a reassuring arm around Pam's shoulders. "You're in expert hands with John."

"Are you a veterinarian, too?"

"No. I came along to lend a hand." Maggie looked toward the kennel area. Dogs barked and howled, and cats meowed in distress. "I can at least provide solace to these poor creatures."

"We can use all the help we can get," the intake staffer said. "I'll assist Dr. ...?" She looked at John.

"John," he said, already striding toward the German shepherd who continued to scratch his blackened ears, yelping in pain at each passing of his paws.

The noisy chorus continued to emanate from the kennel area.

"Let's try to settle them down and get the remaining crates stocked with blankets or towels and water bowls," Pam said to Maggie. "Another group of evacuees will be here in less than thirty minutes."

The two women moved off together.

John set the black duffel full of supplies on the floor at his feet. "Can you stay with me to assist?" He looked at the young woman.

She nodded. "I'm Trisha."

"Do you have any medical training, Trisha?" John rummaged through the supplies in the duffel.

"No, but I'm a senior in college and I'm applying to vet schools next year."

"Tonight should give you a good idea if the profession is what you want." John pulled out a wrapped syringe and a glass vial of a clear liquid. "This guy is by far the worst hurt. I can't get close enough to examine those ears yet, but they may be third-degree burns."

The German shepherd coughed.

"I wouldn't be surprised if he didn't damage his lungs with smoke inhalation. It's common in animals who've been through wildfires." He got onto his knees and held out the back of one hand for the dog to sniff.

"Should I get a muzzle?" Trisha asked. "If he's badly hurt, won't he bite?"

"Let's hold off for now. He didn't bite the van driver who rescued him. Putting a muzzle on him might be necessary, but it'll further traumatize him. I'd like to try to make friends first."

The dog coughed again, so hard that he gagged and vomited.

Trisha hovered over John's shoulder. "Could he be bad enough that we … we have to put him to sleep?"

"Possibly," John replied. "Burns are extremely painful, and lung damage is hard to treat. I won't allow this animal to suffer if I find I can't help him." John extended a finger and gently stroked the dog's muzzle.

The shepherd swiped John's hand with his tongue and thumped his tail against the floor.

John cut his eyes to Trisha. "That tells me this guy wants to live. He's clearly suffering, so I'm going to inject a painkiller to make him more comfortable."

Trisha released the breath she had been holding. "I'm so glad."

John drew the liquid painkiller into the syringe and slowly moved toward the dog. "This is going to make you feel better real soon," John said to his patient. "Once it takes effect, we'll clean you up and figure out what else you need."

The dog thumped his tail again.

"Don't you worry, we're going to take care of you," Trisha said.

John administered the shot. The dog appeared not to notice.

"He tolerated that so well that I'm going to give him

another shot with an antibiotic. He's going to need it, and the sooner we start it, the better."

John produced another syringe and a different vial and gave the shot.

The dog, who had been sitting during these ministrations, now stretched out on the floor.

"The painkiller is taking effect." John addressed Trisha. "I'd like to move him to a sink area where we can flush his damaged skin with water and then dress the wounds. He may need surgery later to debride them, but, for now, we need to get them clean."

"We can take him to the kitchen. There's a stretch of counter space where you can lay him while holding his head over the sink."

"That's exactly what we'll need."

John placed his feet in a wide stance and bent to pick up the half-asleep dog. "There we are." He spoke calmly to the creature, whose only response was to bury his muzzle in John's chest.

Trisha picked up the duffel with medical supplies, and led John to the kitchen where she cleared the counter space to the right of the sink.

John gently lowered the dog into position and turned on the tap to the arched, industrial-style spray nozzle. He tested the water temperature until he was satisfied and began rinsing the burned tissue around the dog's ears, then turned to Trisha. "He's sound asleep. Can you take over for me?"

Trisha nodded her head yes, but her eyes conveyed her doubt.

"All you need to do is to train the water slowly over his burnt ears. The temperature and water pressure I've set is what we need. Support his head and make sure he doesn't become so relaxed that he slips off the counter."

"I can do that."

"Of course you can." John stepped aside and Trisha slipped into place.

"I'm going to bring the other injured dogs from the reception area in here with us. I don't want them out there when the next load of evacuees arrives." He looked around the room and nodded. "This will do nicely as an impromptu emergency room."

"We plan to have a small medical room here at the shelter," Trisha said. "We haven't had time to finish it yet."

"Do you have medical supplies anywhere?"

With her hands full, Trisha used her foot to point to a metal cabinet along one wall of the kitchen. "Everything we have is in there."

"I'd like to hook that guy up to an IV as soon as possible," John said.

"We don't have anything like that."

"I'll text my vet friend and ask him to have someone bring out what we'll need. Your community seems to be full of people willing to help."

"That's Linden Falls for you." Trisha's voice contained more than a note of pride.

"You're doing great," John said. "I'll be right back with the other dogs. We'll have everyone taken care of in no time."

"Maggie?" Pam raised her voice to be heard above the noise in the kennels.

"In here," Maggie called back. She ran her hand down the spine of an oversized mutt of indeterminate origin in a final stroke, planted a kiss on the top of her head, and got to her feet.

"Oh." Pam appeared at the door to the dog run. "I wondered where you'd gone."

"She was clinging to the back of the cage, trembling. Not making a sound. Somehow, that was worse than all the dogs who are whimpering or barking. This poor gal couldn't even voice her feelings." Maggie bent over and stroked her again. "I had to come in here to offer some reassurance."

The dog wagged her tail and walked to Pam to sniff her.

"Looks like you've worked your magic with her. She seems very calm now."

Maggie flushed with pleasure. "I hope you're right."

"I just got a message—the next van has a dozen evacuees and will be here in five minutes—and there's another two vans coming right after that," Pam said.

"Showtime!" Maggie enthusiastically replied.

"Exactly. We've stocked all the crates and kennels with blankets and water. Once we've placed these new animals, you can go home if you want."

Maggie shook her head. "I'll stay as long as John is here. I talked to him briefly when I went to the ladies' room. They've had another half dozen injured strays come in." She and Pam made their way to the reception area and stepped out into the chilly evening to wait for the "incoming."

"How badly injured are they? We're not equipped to be an animal hospital. Heck—until today we weren't really a functioning animal rescue shelter."

"John said all but one of them, so far, have superficial burns. Most of them look like they're family pets. Some of them have collars with name tags."

"Once we get this next batch of animals settled, we should call their owners," Pam said.

"John told me Trisha has already contacted the numbers on all the tags. She had to leave voicemails for most of them, but three people answered their phones and they're all on their way to pick up their pets."

"That's happy news. I hope I get to witness one of those reunions. That'll cheer me up."

"This has been quite a day. We could all use that sort of pick-me-up." Maggie crossed her arms over her chest and rubbed her hands along her arms to warm herself. "John wanted me to ask if you have a device that reads microchips."

"It's on back order," Pam said.

"John suggested if you don't, he'll ask his vet friend to bring the one from his clinic. Reuniting the strays with minor injuries with their owners is best for everyone."

"What about that German shepherd? He looked bad."

"John wants to move him to his friend's clinic tonight. He's afraid the dog has suffered smoke inhalation damage to his lungs and needs robust treatment."

"Poor guy," Pam said.

Headlights cut a swath across the road before them.

"They're here!" Pam stepped to the back of the van when it pulled to a halt. She and Maggie were soon moving between the van and the kennels, situating the nine dogs and six cats.

"No injured strays on that one," Pam called to Maggie as another van came into view.

The next driver reported that the advancing flames had required them to load all remaining animals into his van. He carried a dozen cats and sixteen dogs. They'd had to double up the dogs and put three cats in each crate. He opened the cargo doors at the rear of the van and his charges were eerily silent.

"It's almost as if they understood how close they came to disaster," he told Pam.

Pam and Maggie each grabbed a crate, and the driver followed suit. He helped them situate the last group of evacuees. "I don't believe you have one more spot for any living creature," he said when they were done. He scanned the room. "Looks to me like you are at capacity."

"I think you're right," Pam said. She and Maggie walked the man back to his empty van.

His taillights were a receding red glow when another set of headlights illuminated the driveway into the shelter.

"OMG," Pam said. "Not more?!"

"It's not a van," Maggie said. "That's a sedan."

Pam and Maggie waited on the walkway to the front door as a Prius pulled up in front of them. The car had barely stopped moving when a woman jumped out of the driver's seat, followed by two young girls from the back seat.

"Do you have a dachshund here?" The woman rushed to Pam and Maggie. "He's a traditional brown and tan doxie—a bit overweight—with a red collar and name tag? Wally?"

"Did you get a call that he's here?" Pam asked.

The girls had joined their mother and velcroed themselves to her legs on either side. All three of them nodded vigorously in the affirmative.

"Then I'm sure we do," Pam said.

The girls both burst into tears.

"Follow me," Pam said and led them into the reception area.

"Looks like we're going to witness that gleeful reunion of pet and owner," Maggie whispered to Pam.

Pam raised an eyebrow at Maggie and nodded. "Wait here with Maggie," she said to the mother and daughters. "I'll bring Wally to you."

Maggie asked if they'd like to sit while they waited, but they declined.

After what seemed like an eternity, Pam appeared at the end of the hall, being dragged by a determined dachshund at the end of a leash.

When the dog saw his family, he kicked his legs into turbo gear.

Pam lost her grip on the leash and Wally sailed down the tile hallway, his paws barely hitting the ground.

The girls dropped to their knees as Wally propelled himself into their arms.

Pam joined Maggie to watch the heartwarming scene. It was impossible to tell who was wriggling faster and giving out more kisses—Wally or the girls.

Maggie put her arm around Pam's waist and leaned into her. "You were so right. This is exactly what I needed to see tonight."

CHAPTER 3

Sunday Sloan marked the spot in *The New York Times* bestselling thriller she was reading with a bookmark. As a librarian, and one with a specialty in rare books, she had too much reverence for books to (*shudder*) fold over the corner of the page. She placed the book on the coffee table in front of her and stretched, her toes curled into the thick rug and her arms reaching for the ceiling.

Josh Newlon sat at her kitchen table, typing furiously on his laptop. Pages torn from a yellow legal pad surrounded him and post-it notes circled the edge of his computer screen, like moths drawn to a flame.

Sunday rose and came to stand behind him. She massaged his shoulders.

Josh leaned back against her and placed his left hand over hers. "Gosh—that feels good."

"Your shoulders are so tense. You've been hunched over

that laptop since right after dinner. It's eleven and you're still hard at it."

He shut his laptop and stood. "I want all this applying for jobs stuff to be over with. Filling out applications, attaching references, and answering questions for jobs in college administration is almost as detailed as applying for a slot in a master's degree program in the field."

"Searching for jobs in academia is cumbersome," she agreed. "That's one reason I was beyond thrilled to be offered a librarian job at Highpointe. I figured I could spend my entire career here and never have to apply again." She planted a kiss on the top of his head. "Still, you must be excited about graduating soon."

"I'm ready to be done with being a starving student," he said. "But unless I get a job, I'll be unemployed and starving."

"It won't come to that," Sunday said. "You'll find something—and it'll be great." She swallowed hard and didn't say what she was thinking. She wanted—more than anything—for Josh to get a job at Highpointe and stay here, in Westbury, with her.

"I've submitted for six open positions at Highpointe," Josh said, as if he could read his girlfriend's mind. "I really thought I'd have heard something by now."

"Have you asked Maggie about them?"

"No. As Highpointe's president, I'm sure she'd have the influence to get me hired. I don't want to land a position because she's pulled strings for me."

Sunday bit her lip. That's how people got jobs all the time. *It's called networking,* she thought.

"I want to start my professional career by securing a position on my own merits." He began gathering up the stacks of yellow paper and shoved them into his backpack. "That's why I spent all evening applying for jobs that I would love—if they were only in Westbury."

The eyes he turned to her—besides fatigued—were now full of longing and desire.

Sunday walked him to her door and slid her arms around his waist. She pulled him close. "Things will work out exactly as they're supposed to," she said. "I think you'll find the perfect opportunity right here." She hoped she sounded more convincing than she felt.

CHAPTER 4

Maggie checked her watch for the hundredth time, then opened the airline's app on her phone. Their flight still showed that it was on time and boarding would start in forty-five minutes. She held out her screen to John and bit her lip.

John leaned forward from the back seat of the cab that inched ahead in bumper-to-bumper traffic and tapped on the plexiglass divider.

The cabbie slid the window open.

"How much longer until we get to JFK?"

"We should be past the accident that's holding everything up in another five minutes. After that, it'll be clear sailing. I'll drop you at your terminal in thirty minutes. Maybe forty."

Maggie's hand, holding the phone, dropped to her lap like a stone.

John rocked back into his seat and turned to her. "I'm sorry, sweetheart. We're going to miss our plane."

"You had nothing to do with this accident," Maggie said, moderating her tone. The accident wasn't his fault, but he'd been the one to push back their flight by a day so he could stay in Linden Falls to assist at his friend's clinic, again as a "veterinary technician."

"If we'd left yesterday afternoon, as planned, we'd have woken up in our own bed this morning. I suggested we change our flights and leave late Sunday morning. That already put us getting home later than we like when we both have to work tomorrow." He looked into her eyes. "I feel terrible about this."

"Don't be ridiculous. Stan said you were a godsend to him and those poor animals. Staying was the right thing to do—if you hadn't suggested it, I would have."

"You mean that?"

"I do."

"You're not secretly ready to kill me?" He held her gaze. "Because I can tell you're annoyed."

"You know me so well. I'm always upset when things don't go as planned." Maggie laughed and turned her head aside. "I'm not the most flexible person when unexpected things throw a monkey wrench into my schedule. That doesn't mean that I'm not glad we stayed on." She looked at her watch again. "We still haven't cleared the accident, and it's been more than five minutes. Our flight is going to leave without us. Since we're just sitting here, I'll call the airline to rebook our flight."

After waiting on hold for ten minutes, Maggie finally got through to a person. While listening to the man go through the flights that weren't already fully booked, the cab merged into the lane that snaked by a multi-car pileup and resumed highway speed. Maggie relayed their two choices to John: one flight would leave in an hour and forty-five minutes and get them home at dinnertime. The other flight wouldn't leave for another four hours and they'd be lucky to walk in their front door by 9:30 p.m.

"We're moving now," John said. "We can make the earlier flight. That gets us home later than we'd like, as it is. I don't want to delay any more than we have to."

"We'd save money on the later flight," Maggie said.

"I don't care about that. Do you?"

Maggie shook her head and booked the seats for the mid-afternoon flight.

The cab deposited them at their terminal five minutes after their first flight had departed. They checked their bags at the curb—including the extra suitcase they'd had to purchase to transport the table linens Maggie had purchased—before the wildfire occurred—at the charming farmers market booth run by Pam's mother.

The porter handed them their baggage claim tickets and told them their gate number. He informed them that their flight was delayed by thirty minutes.

John groaned.

"It's only thirty minutes," Maggie said. "Let's go find something to eat. I'm hungry."

They proceeded to their gate and checked the departure board. Their flight was still delayed by thirty minutes.

"We passed an area with three or four restaurants, a coffee shop, and a fast-food franchise," John said. "We'll have time to eat, thanks to this delay."

"Okay, Pollyanna." Maggie smiled at her husband. "I'm glad you're looking on the bright side."

"I'm trying. It won't do us any good if we're both upset."

"Does that mean I can be grumpy?" Maggie asked. "Because I'm having a hard time pushing down my impatience."

John put his arm around her shoulders and steered her toward the food court. "I hereby grant you permission to be as crabby as you want."

"Thank you. I feel better already," Maggie sarcastically quipped.

"On one condition," John said.

Maggie arched her brows at him.

"You don't use this delay as an excuse to pull out your laptop and start catching up on your emails."

"But…"

John held up a hand to stop her. "No buts. We both agreed we'd unplug until Monday morning. We've honored that agreement until now, and I don't think jumping into your busy inbox is going to improve your mood."

"Probably not," Maggie reluctantly agreed. "But we've got all this extra time. May as well put it to good use."

"Didn't you bring a book club book with you?"

"I finished it yesterday while you were at the clinic."

They walked past a shop that sold an astounding array of NYC souvenirs and arrived at the area where several restaurants were clustered.

They scanned the posted menus and John suggested the one offering burgers and fries. "A decent hamburger always cheers my girl up," he teased.

She patted his back. "As if you're not a fan, too."

"That I am." He pointed down the concourse. "Is that what I think it is?"

Maggie looked in the direction he was pointing. "A bookstore!"

"Do you know the next book you're reading for book club?"

"Yes. And it's on *The New York Times* bestseller list. They'll carry it there. I'm excited to read it."

"That's perfect, then. We'll have a delicious lunch…"

Maggie rolled her eyes at him.

"And you can read all afternoon. I think that would constitute a perfect Sunday if we were home."

Maggie stood on her tiptoes and kissed his cheek. "You're exactly right, Mr. Allen. Thank you for pushing the reset button on my attitude."

John flushed with pleasure. "Always here to help."

∽

JOHN TURNED his large SUV onto the long, winding driveway leading up the hill to Rosemont. Tall trees cast thin shadows across the warm limestone walls. The windows of the attic on the third floor rose above the tree line and glimmered in the pale moonlight.

John drove past the stone steps leading to the arched, mahogany front door. The large pendent light over the covered entry glowed a warm welcome home.

"We're here," he said, glancing over at Maggie. Her head had dropped to her chest for the last twenty minutes of their drive home.

Maggie snapped her head up and pushed her hair off her face. "Did I nod off?"

"Afraid so."

"I'm sorry, John. I meant to stay awake—to help you stay alert for the hour-long drive home from the airport."

He pulled around the side of the stately manor home to the four-car garage added to the house decades earlier. "I managed just fine," he said, "but, now that we're home, I'm ready to collapse."

He parked in the garage, and they got out of the car. "It's almost one," Maggie said. "I can't believe our flight kept getting delayed. We would have been better off if we'd have booked the later flight in the first place."

John opened the hatchback and began removing their luggage. "I know. It took off before ours did. Oh, well—we're home now."

Maggie extended the handle on one of her suitcases, piled her carry-on and a duffel on top, and rolled the precarious bundle into their house.

John followed behind with the rest of the luggage, and Maggie disarmed their home alarm.

"I'm too tired to deal with any of this tonight," she said, dumping her load at the base of the stairs. "I'm going straight upstairs. If I can stay awake long enough to brush my teeth and change into my pajamas, I'll be amazed."

John deposited the rest of their luggage next to hers. "I'm going to leave a voicemail for Sherry that I won't be at the animal hospital until mid-morning and ask that she carry the load until I get there."

"Good idea." Maggie extended her hand to him, and he took it. Together, they wearily trudged up the stairs. "I told Josh not to schedule anything for me before noon. I planned to use Monday morning to catch up on email—not my sleep."

"Stuff happens," John said. "The only thing we can do now is fall into bed and get some sleep."

Maggie and John did just that.

Maggie slowly opened one eye the next morning. The sound of running water from the bathroom told her John was taking a shower. Sun was streaming through a crack in the heavy drapes drawn across the tall, mullioned windows overlooking Rosemont's back lawn.

She pushed herself onto her elbows and looked at her bedside clock. It was almost ten. She'd slept much later than she'd expected. Maggie threw off the duvet and flung herself out of bed. She'd grab her cosmetic bag so she could shower, put on her face, and get out the door as soon as possible.

Maggie headed for the staircase. There—neatly lined up in the middle of the hallway—was their luggage. All of their luggage.

"How odd," she murmured. John must have brought it up before he got in the shower. He must have done that while he was waiting for the water to get hot.

She picked up her cosmetic bag and was headed back to their room when the smell of freshly brewed coffee wafted up from the first floor. The heavenly aroma stopped her dead in her tracks. Her husband was a marvel. How had she gotten so lucky? It smelled like he'd used freshly ground beans, too.

Maggie abandoned her makeup case and raced down the stairs. The least she could do for this wonder of a husband of hers was to bring him a cup of coffee.

By the time Maggie returned to their bedroom, carrying two steamy cups of coffee, John had finished his shower.

He stood, wrapped in a towel, leaning over the sink, shaving.

Maggie placed his mug on the counter next to his sink.

"That's so nice of you," John said at the same time that Maggie was saying, "I can't believe you did this."

They looked at each other in some confusion. "You brought the luggage upstairs and started the coffee before you got in the shower," Maggie said.

John shook his head. "No. It was so late when I woke up that I got right in the shower."

Maggie stared at him blankly.

"You made the coffee," he stated.

It was her turn to shake her head no. "I didn't bring the luggage upstairs, either."

John tilted his head to one side and narrowed his eyes to slits. "I'm too tired for practical jokes."

"I'm not the one joking," Maggie replied, punching his biceps playfully.

"If one of us isn't playing a trick on the other," he said, "then maybe there is some truth to the old tale that Rosemont is haunted."

"You mean by that butler who worked here for over fifty years? What was his name?"

"Alistair."

"Yes. I remember now."

"It must have been Alistair," John said.

"At least he's a friendly, helpful ghost," Maggie said. "If you won't admit you did these nice things, then it must have been him."

John picked up his mug and took a sip of coffee.

Maggie raised her mug and clinked it against his. "Here's to Alistair," she said. "May he always feel welcome at Rosemont."

CHAPTER 5

Maggie met Josh in the corridor outside her office.

"Good. You're here," he said, his tone slightly breathless. He changed directions and walked with her into the reception area outside her office.

"Good morning to you, too," Maggie chided.

"Sorry. Good morning. It's already been quite a day—and it's only 10:45." The phone on his desk started ringing.

"What's going on?" Maggie raised an eyebrow.

Josh hurried to the insistent phone. He gestured to Maggie's office with his head. "Susan's waiting for you. She'll fill you in."

Maggie's bemusement at Josh's harried state segued into alarm. Her daughter should be at her law practice in the middle of a Monday morning, not camped out in Maggie's office.

Maggie pushed through the door to her large, presidential-looking office. Susan Scanlon sat at the round conference table in front of a wall of tall windows, hunched over her laptop.

"Hey, Mom." Susan finished the sentence she was writing, then closed her computer and rose to greet her mother with a hug.

Maggie embraced her daughter lightly, then stepped back. "What's going on? You never come here in the middle of the day."

"Let's sit down." Susan guided her mother to one of the wing-backed chairs in front of Maggie's desk. Susan lowered herself into the other chair.

"Now you're scaring me," Maggie said. Her hand gripped the arm of her chair. "Is something wrong with you or Aaron? Or Julia?"

"No. Nothing like that."

"Mike or Amy or the twins?"

Susan shook her head. "The family is fine." She narrowed her eyes. "Have you heard any news this morning?"

"No. Our flight didn't get in until after eleven last night. It was almost one when we got home. John and I collapsed into bed and slept in. Fortunately, I had nothing on my calendar until after lunch. I woke up late, showered, and got here as fast as I could."

"No news in the car?"

"Just the BBC World Service Newshour."

Susan blew out a breath. "At least this story isn't international news. Not yet."

"What's going on? Tell me."

"Do you remember Dad's college president buddy? Malcolm Yates."

"Yes. I only met him a couple of times at conferences where the wives tagged along. Funny you should mention him. He and his wife were at the conference I spoke at recently as a last-minute stand-in for a panelist who had to back out."

"Did you talk to them?"

"Not really. I didn't see him at all. His wife attended my session and asked some snippy questions during the Q&A about your father's embezzlement."

Susan leaned forward, almost falling out of her chair, her back ramrod straight. "You didn't tell me this." Her tone was accusatory.

Maggie shrugged. "It was unnerving at the time, but nothing came of it. The moderator of the panel shut her down fast. No one else in the room seemed to know or care what she was talking about. Frankly," Maggie looked into Susan's eyes, "I forgot all about it."

Susan nodded and studied her hands, deep in thought.

"Susan ... tell me!"

"Malcolm is the talk of the news cycle today." Susan swiveled her face to her mother's. "It seems a professor at his college made a formal complaint against him, alleging that he solicited sexual favors from her in exchange for his support of her being granted tenure."

Maggie slammed back in her chair as if she'd been

speeding down the highway and suddenly applied the brakes. "That's bad."

"There's more. Since the first allegation surfaced several weeks ago, additional women have come forward. Professors, interns, students, staff. Honestly, Mom—I don't know how he found the time to harass all of them."

"That's despicable."

"And criminal. The police arrested him this morning. All the news outlets covered it. He was dragged out of his house in handcuffs around six this morning. His wife was at their front door in her bathrobe, nearly hysterical."

Maggie inhaled sharply. "I can see why."

"Having your husband be the newest poster child for the Me Too movement would suck."

"I always found her to be uppity and aloof when I ran into her at conferences back in the day. And she was positively obnoxious at that conference recently, but I wouldn't wish what's happening to her now on anybody." Maggie shook her head slowly. "I can't believe I'm saying this, but I feel sorry for Yolanda Yates."

"I thought this would be your reaction. You're an empathetic person."

"What's the harm in that?"

"Normally nothing, but this situation might be different."

"Why would *that* be?"

Susan drew a deep breath and held it for a few seconds before continuing. "The news outlets are showing an old photo of Yates—taken in a bar somewhere—with two of his college president buddies. All three men have their arms around the shoulders of markedly younger women."

Maggie moved her right hand to clutch the strand of pearls at her neck. Her eyes telegraphed fear and disbelief. "No..."

Susan closed her eyes and moved her head in a shallow nod. "I'm afraid so. Dad was in that picture."

Maggie choked as she cursed.

"That's why I came in to wait for you. If you'd have seen the news, you would have called me."

Maggie's breaths were uneven.

"You're going to have to see that picture, Mom, and listen to all the news stories. I'm going to be right beside you while you do."

"Oh, honey. He was your father. You don't have to..."

"Yes, I do. Did you notice how frazzled Josh was when you came in this morning?"

"He seemed a bit harried."

"That's because every news reporter in the country is calling you—asking for a statement, wanting an interview. Was Paul Martin unfaithful? Did he harass women like his buddy, Malcolm? Did you know about Yates?"

Maggie groaned. "I didn't know about any of it—regarding either Malcolm or Paul. I can't throw light on anything."

"You'll have to make a statement. Today. I may be an attorney, but I'm also your daughter. I won't represent you, but I can help you hire a fabulous team. You'll need a PR firm and an attorney who specializes in defamation."

Maggie pressed her palms to the sides of her head. "I can't believe this." She turned to Susan. "You're right. Can you give me names to call?"

"I've done better than that. We've got an appointment with the top PR firm in the region at one today. The attorney they recommend will be there, too." She searched her mother's face. "Are you ready to delve into the news?"

"I believe I need to, ready or not."

"We'll watch it on my laptop." Susan stood, and they moved to the conference table. The second video clip from a network news morning show was playing when Josh tapped lightly on the door to the office.

"That'll be Josh," Susan said. "I instructed him to tell everyone you weren't available. Come in," she called.

Josh poked his head around the door. "The chairman of Highpointe's board of trustees has called and left messages six times," he said.

"Did you follow the script I gave you?" Susan asked.

"Yes. To the letter. He said if you didn't call him within the hour, Maggie, he's going to drive over here and demand an answer." Josh swiped the perspiration from his brow.

"This must be hard on you, Josh. I'm sorry we've put you in such a difficult position," Maggie said.

"Don't worry about me. I'm fine. I wanted you to know … in case you have somewhere else you need to be."

"As a matter of fact, we do," Susan said. She shut her laptop. "We can finish watching this at my office. The PR firm is in the next building," she said to Maggie before turning back to Josh. "Tell the chairman—or any of the trustees—that the college and Ms. Martin, individually, are making no comment to the press. Ms. Martin will be in touch to address their concerns by the end of the day."

"Got it," Josh said, retreating with urgency to the reception area and the phone ringing on his desk.

"The attorney and PR firm will advise you on what to say to the trustees, too. Your best course of action is to maintain your silence until you've met with your advisors."

"I like the sound of that," Maggie said. "I need to tell John—to warn him in case reporters come to the animal hospital."

"I've already talked to his practice manager. He was with a patient. She said they haven't seen any press and I told her what to do and say if they turn up." Susan inserted her laptop in her satchel and stepped to the window. "There is, however, a gaggle of reporters by the main entrance here. I'm glad I parked behind the building."

"You are a clever girl." Maggie grinned at her resourceful daughter. "I'm thankful you're on my side."

"Let's slip out the back before anyone stakes out the rear of the building." Susan grasped her mother's elbow, and they made their escape without being noticed.

∽

"I THINK THAT'S EVERYTHING," Maggie said, logging off of her computer. She and Susan had returned to Maggie's office after their lengthy meeting with the PR team and their lawyer.

"Let me review my notes of our meeting with the team," Susan said. She ticked off items on a list as she moved her pen down a page on a legal pad. "You've participated in a Zoom meeting with the board, and they issued a press release recommended by the lawyer affirming the college's ethics policy regarding harassment and disavowing any connection with Yates. I'm gratified that the chairman added the section praising you and your initiatives to increase Highpointe's outreach to older adult students and highlighting your exceptional financial management."

"Frankly, that amazed me," Maggie said. "I didn't expect a pat on the back."

"Long overdue and well deserved, if you ask me," Susan said.

Maggie took over itemizing the afternoon's progress. "My personal statement went out saying that I endorse Highpointe's policies, that I don't know any of the people making allegations against Yates, I've never seen the photo of my husband with Yates, and I don't know any of the women in the photo."

"It's wise to communicate only in writing. There's nothing to be gained by holding a press conference."

"I'm glad the PR team insisted on preparing everything that will go out from me," Maggie said. "I'm hoping this will all blow over for us. Yates will be a different story. As it should be."

She pulled her purse off the back of her chair and stood.

Susan gathered her papers and stowed them in her satchel.

They moved to the door to Maggie's office, and Maggie paused, her hand on the handle. "Can I ask you something?"

"Sure."

"Did that young woman in the photo with your dad look familiar to you?"

"No. And the pose didn't look sexual, either. His hand was touching the center of her back. He wasn't pulling her close to him. Nothing of the sort. He might have been photographed with me in exactly the same way."

Maggie smiled at her daughter. She still wanted to believe that her father was a good man.

"Why? Do you recognize her?"

Maggie shrugged, then shook her head. "I honestly don't know. The photo was taken at least twenty years ago. I met so many people during our time at Windsor College."

"She's a pretty, young blonde woman. That describes fifty percent of the coeds in Southern California."

"That must be it. Paul's been dead for many years now, so I guess we'll never know."

They stepped out of the office to find Josh busy at his desk in the reception area.

"What are you still doing here, Josh?" Maggie asked. "I thought you were going to get out of here as soon as you sent out the press release from the board of trustees. That went out at six-thirty. It's now almost eight."

"I know," he said, tearing his eyes from his laptop. "I've been doing my homework."

"Why are you working on it here?"

"I wanted to stay to walk the two of you to your cars. If there are still any reporters out there, I'll chase them off."

Maggie smiled for the first time that day. "That's very thoughtful of you, Josh."

"Chivalrous, even," Susan chimed in.

"Nobody's going to mess with the two of you on my watch," he said. He placed his laptop in his backpack and walked Maggie and Susan to the parking lot.

"It looks like those press statements did the trick," Maggie said. "Nobody's waiting to ambush us to get an exclusive."

Susan spun around. "You're right."

"Maybe today was just a tempest in a teapot," Maggie said.

"We can hope." Susan yawned and stretched. "I'm headed home. With any luck, I'll be there before Julia goes to bed. I'm going to turn in as soon as she does." She leaned in and gave her mother a half hug. "Call me if anything comes up."

"Will do," Maggie said. "I don't know what I'd do without you, sweetheart. Thank you."

Susan waved a hand in dismissal of her mother's words of gratitude and headed for her car.

Maggie looked at Josh. "Thank you for devoting your day to taking care of me. I'm blessed to have you in my corner."

"Always," Josh said.

They arrived at Maggie's car, and Josh held the door open for her.

"Why don't you come in late tomorrow? I think you've earned a perk."

"That's generous of you, but unnecessary."

"Or another time when it might be helpful to have some extra time off."

"Well—if you really mean it—I was going to ask for time off during the week of Halloween."

"Sure."

"Halloween is Robert's favorite holiday," A warm smile appeared on Josh's face as he mentioned Robert Harris, his biological father who he'd recently been reunited with. "He goes all out decorating their place. I've been helping him put up lights and erect a haunted house for the past two weekends. He says there'll be a lot of last-minute things to do that week."

"By all means," Maggie said. "Take the entire day off."

"Thanks. Robert will be thrilled." He began to move away from her car, then turned back. "Be sure to tell Susan to bring Julia to trick-or-treat. Robert has a little, kid-friendly maze open until eight o'clock and brings out the scary animatronics for the big kids after that. You should see it. The man's a genius with Halloween decorations."

"I'll tell her. You should alert the Westbury Gazette, too. They might want to send out a reporter."

"Thanks, I'll have to think about that," Josh said. "After today's experience, I may have had my fill of reporters. See you in the morning."

CHAPTER 6

Josh arrived at his parents' home early on the morning of October 29. He'd stopped at Laura's bakery on the way for a box of her legendary pumpkin spice muffins. Sunday claimed they were her favorite thing about fall in Westbury. She'd made the trip to Laura's twice in the last week during her lunch hour, only to find that Laura was sold out.

He lifted the lid of the pink bakery box and removed two of the muffins. He wrapped them in the thin parchment paper that lined the box and placed them on the passenger seat. Satisfied that the surprise treats for Sunday were secure, he headed for the house with the rest of the muffins.

He'd always admired the solid brick structure with the wrap-around porch, but now that he had connected with his birth parents and they lived here, the place occupied a special place in his heart. His parents had been separated before he was born but had been reunited recently in the most extraordinary circumstance. Remembering all that had happened still brought him close to tears.

The front door banged open before Josh reached the steps to the porch.

"There you are, my boy," Robert boomed, his dignified British accent full of good cheer. "Come inside. I've got a full English breakfast waiting for you. If we're going to break our backs today, we'll do it properly nourished."

"You're in fine fettle today." He lifted the bakery box. "Can we add Laura's muffins to our breakfast?"

"Heavens, yes. We can always add anything from her bakery. That woman is a genius. If she lived in the UK, she'd be a shoo-in for star baker on *The Great British Baking Show*."

Josh climbed the steps and Robert put his arm around his son's shoulders as they walked to the kitchen.

"Is Lyla up yet?"

"At the crack of dawn. She left for work as soon as she could get herself dressed. Said she didn't want to get caught up in the frenzy of Halloween decor madness that she thinks will take place here today."

"I'm afraid she might have a point." Josh swiveled to Robert. "Your garage is full of stuff that we've got to set up today. You must have bought every inflatable decoration and animatronic sold at a big box home improvement center within a fifty-mile radius."

Robert cleared his throat. "I admit—I might have gone a bit overboard. I've always loved Halloween. Being a rare book expert, I've been around legions of spooky classics my entire life. You Americans go all out for this holiday. I'm so happy to be married to your mother finally—and to know you most especially ..." His voice cracked, and he took a steadying breath. "Well, I just let myself lean into it. Isn't that the term these days?"

Josh chuckled. "That's understandable. But seriously—you can't even park in the garage anymore."

"Ah!" Robert held up his right hand and pointed to the ceiling. "Easy solution. I've leased a storage unit. I'll rent a truck and take all of this there next week. You won't have to help. I can manage on my own."

"No way am I going to let you do that."

"Thanks, son," Robert said. "Now, we've got both bacon and sausages, eggs, fried tomatoes, toast, and baked beans. I've made coffee and tea. Let's tuck in while I show you my diagram of what's going to go where."

∽

FUELED BY THE FORTIFYING BREAKFAST, Robert and Josh took thermal mugs of tea and coffee, respectively, out to the garage. Josh stood in the driveway while Robert activated the door opener.

"Am I seeing things, or are there two new animatronics in there?" Josh put his free hand on top of his head. "You didn't have that huge flying dragon last weekend."

Robert shrugged. "It was half price yesterday."

Josh walked up to the dragon to examine it. "Good call. This is my favorite—it's awesome."

Robert pointed to the bales of hay stacked along one side of the garage. "We'll build our little-kid maze with these on the front lawn. It'll be six feet high. If anyone taller than six feet goes in the maze, they'll have to duck."

"We're stretching tarps across the top, right?" Josh asked.

Robert nodded. "We'll string fairy lights inside and hang plastic bats and ghosts from the ceiling. They're in those dollar-store bags." He pointed. "I've also got plastic spiders to put along the walls."

Josh opened the bags. "The bats are fine, and the ghosts look friendly, but these spiders are very realistic. They may be too creepy for tiny kids."

"You think?"

"I honestly have no idea."

Father and son looked at each other.

"Lyla's coming home for lunch. She's bringing us sandwiches. We'll ask her what she thinks."

"Good idea. She'll know. We don't want to terrify anyone."

"That's why we're going to put tarps over some of the animatronics after we put them in place. We'll pull them off at eight o'clock. The older kids will love them."

"All the animatronics are terrifying," Josh said. "Even the small dog and cat ones. Those glowing red eyes are … unnerving. I'm bringing Dan with me on Halloween, but he's staying inside. He may be a hundred-pound black Lab, but he's a big baby."

"I'll tell people to come back after eight for the full display," Robert said.

"Let's post signs to that effect, too."

"Brilliant!" Robert rubbed his hands together. "Let's get started. Nobody's going to see any of this if it remains in the garage."

"I hope you've got a ton of candy. Word will get out and everyone in town will come by."

"Lyla said the same thing. She's planning to buy more."

"I can't wait," Josh said.

"Neither can I."

CHAPTER 7

John tapped the screen to end his call and turned to the dogs curled up on their memory foam dog beds in front of the library fireplace. "We've got to go tell Maggie," he said to them.

Roman, his golden retriever, lifted his head, but Eve, Maggie's terrier-mix rescue dog, remained motionless, with her nose tucked under her tail.

"Where's your mommy?" John's voice was as much an invitation as a question. "Let's go find her."

Roman stood and gave himself a good shake. The motion woke Eve, who cracked open one eye to see if she really needed to get up.

"Come on," John commanded as he slapped his thigh.

Eve stretched her paws in front of her before reluctantly getting to her feet.

John led them into the adjacent living room. There was

no sign of Maggie, and the rest of the rooms on the first floor were dark. The chandelier on the sweeping staircase to the second floor illuminated the area. Its cut glass prisms sent rainbows cascading down the stairs.

Roman and Eve raced ahead, and John followed. When the dogs got to the second floor, they headed down the hallway to the left instead of turning right to race into the master bedroom suite. They reached an unadorned wooden door that stood propped open by a heavy iron doorstop. The dogs stopped at the open door, wagging their tails vigorously but unwilling to climb the steep stairs to Rosemont's rustic attic.

John joined the dogs. "I should have known," he told them. "Maggie told me yesterday that she wanted to get the inflatable ghost down from the attic for tomorrow night. That means that I'm supposed to come up here to get it. Only I forgot."

He put one foot on the bottom step.

Roman whined plaintively.

"It's okay, boy. You can both stay here. I don't blame you. This attic is spooky—especially after dark." John climbed the stairs and stepped into the crowded attic, dimly lit by two naked overhead bulbs.

Maggie was in the far corner, her back to him, digging through an enormous old cabinet filled with pieces of vintage sterling silver.

"Hi, sweetheart," he said. "What are you doing?"

Maggie pulled a tray out of the way with her left hand and removed a water pitcher from the cabinet with her right.

She turned to John. "There," she said. "This is what I was after." She held up the pitcher. "I thought it was still in the attic, but it took some concerted searching to find it." She sneezed mightily.

John stared at her. "Is there a reason that you suddenly needed that pitcher—at this time of night?"

Maggie chuckled. "I want to polish it before bedtime." She sneezed again and picked her way through the jumble of furniture, boxes, and attic detritus that had accumulated over the years.

"We've got to get this attic cleared out. I'll email Gordon Mortimer tomorrow to find out when he can finish appraising all this stuff." She joined John and held the pitcher up to one of the light bulbs. "Look at the lines of this piece. The curve of the handle is so graceful. It'll be gorgeous once I've cleaned it up."

"I'm sure it will." John put his hand on her waist. "I didn't realize we had an emergency need for a silver pitcher."

Maggie laughed. "It's not for us. I'm going to send it to Pam and Steve—that delightful couple we met in Linden Falls. You remember them?"

John nodded. "Of course. We worked shoulder-to-shoulder with them on the night all those pets were evacuated to the new shelter. They were the hosts of that home improvement TV show that built the shelter."

"Yes. They were getting married the Saturday after we left town. I want to send them this as a wedding present from us."

"That's incredibly thoughtful," John said.

"I got in touch with Paige today. She runs the postal counter in Linden Falls. I'll send it to her, and she'll get it to Pam and Steve."

"You're remarkable." John planted a kiss on the top of Maggie's head.

"If I have time tomorrow, I'll stop by Celebrations. Judy will have something lovely that I can buy to send with this. I'll purchase something from her shop and ask her to wrap and mail it all for us." She turned toward the stairs. "I found the blow-up ghost, too." She pointed to a box sitting to the left of the stairs.

"I'll get that," John said. He bent and picked up the box.

The doors to the cabinet where Maggie had just been rummaging banged shut with a thwack.

Maggie and John looked at each other.

"There aren't any drafts in here," Maggie said.

"I know. Maybe the floor isn't level in that part of the attic and the doors were slowly swinging shut until they got some momentum going?" He shrugged.

"Or maybe Alistair is up here and closed it for us."

They both glanced at the cabinet. It stood in the dim shadows, a faint cloud of dust settling around it.

"That's as good an explanation as any," John said.

They made their way down the stairs.

Roman and Eve waited quietly in the hallway, keeping their eyes trained on the open door until John removed the door stop and shut it firmly.

Maggie led the way to the kitchen. She placed the pitcher on the counter and retrieved the jar of silver polish from under the sink.

"We came looking for you upstairs because we have news," John said.

"Oh?" Maggie rinsed the pitcher, scooped a large dollop of the pinkish paste onto the spongy applicator, and set to her task.

"I texted Stan today to ask how everything's been going with the animals we treated and the shelters—and Linden Falls itself."

"Good. I've been wondering."

"He just called. We didn't lose any animals."

Maggie turned her face to his. "I'm relieved to hear that."

"Do you remember the German shepherd who came in with the first wave of evacuees?"

"I sure do. You were worried he wouldn't make it."

He was microchipped and has been reunited with his owners."

"*That's* happy news."

"The fire just missed Linden Falls but destroyed a tiny town to the west."

"Oh, no! I'm so sorry for those people. Losing your home to a fire is devastating. How about that other shelter—the one they evacuated?"

"It sustained quite a bit of damage, but it's almost ready to reopen. Stan told me the volunteers who built Fur Friends Sanctuary moved right over to Friends Fur Life and had the repairs done in no time."

"I love hearing that. Linden Falls sounds a lot like Westbury."

"Yep. It's a place where people help each other—without being asked."

Maggie rinsed the foamy polish from the pitcher and held it out to John. "Did I miss a spot?"

He grabbed the dish towel from its hook and dried the pitcher, polishing it until it gleamed.

"Now *that's* gorgeous," Maggie said, admiring the piece.

"Do people use silver water pitchers anymore? I've never seen us use one."

"I use mine as vases," Maggie said. "This will be beautiful with either fresh or silk flowers. I hope she loves it."

"I'm sure she will. She's never going to expect a wedding present from us." He set the pitcher down and pulled Maggie into his arms. "You're one classy gal."

Maggie slid her arms up his back, and they kissed until Eve jumped up against Maggie's leg.

"I think these guys want to go out and then head upstairs to bed." Maggie pulled back from John.

"That's a great idea," John said. "I'm pooped. I'm starting my day an hour earlier tomorrow so I can be home when Julia stops by to trick-or-treat."

Maggie pulled her jacket from the coat rack by the back door and slung it around her shoulders. She and John stepped into the crisp night air as the dogs raced ahead down the sloping back lawn.

"That little girl is the apple of your eye, isn't she?"

"I have to admit it—I'm completely smitten. I never

thought I'd get to experience being a grandfather. And then I met you."

Maggie leaned back against his chest, and he circled her with his arms, resting his chin on the top of her head. They stood in silence as thin clouds shrouded the moon, painting the trees at the bottom of the slope with a milky wash.

Roman was the first to return to them, followed by Eve, running hard but hampered by her much shorter legs.

John squatted to pet the smaller dog. "And if you hadn't adopted Maggie on her first night at Rosemont, she wouldn't have needed a veterinarian, and I wouldn't have met her." He tousled Eve's ears. "So, I have you to thank, Eve, for bringing us together and for my being a grandpa."

Maggie's heart turned over, as it always did, when she looked at the remarkable man she'd married—and their two sweet dogs. "I think Eve brought unimaginable joy into my life, too."

John stood, and the four of them headed up the stairs to their beds.

CHAPTER 8

Alistair:
Today was the big day: Halloween.

I floated downstairs after Maggie and John left for work. Roman greeted me with a thump of his tail. Eve remained curled in a ball on her bed by the living room hearth, but she kept her eyes open and trained on me. She wasn't scared or upset by my presence—just curious.

I nodded in their direction and headed for the pantry. I'd spent hours in this generous room off the kitchen when I'd been Rosemont's butler. It seemed like ages ago—probably because it had been ages ago.

I'd been the last butler in residence at Rosemont. The thought made me sad. A grand house like Rosemont deserved a butler. That I was a mere ghost of my formal self (*I paused to chuckle at my witticism*) shouldn't matter. As of today, I was going to act like a butler—at least as much as possible in my condition.

The pantry was tidy, with rows of glassware and stacks of plates on shelves. I got close enough to note the fine layer of dust along the top two shelves. I'd never have allowed such a thing in my day.

Odd-looking contraptions lined the countertop. The only thing they had in common was a short, black, rubbery rope that was attached to them at one end and had a rectangular blob of rubber from which two metal prongs protruded at the other end. We'd had a toaster with a similar cord in my day, but I couldn't tell if any of these gadgets was a modern-day toaster.

I continued my search and found two large shopping bags at the far end of the room. They both contained bags of candy. Bingo. That proved we were ready for the Halloween tradition of trick-or-treat.

My next stop was the foyer, and I soon found what I was searching for. The box with the inflatable ghost sat by the front door, its contents spilling out onto the floor. The face of this ghost wasn't a grotesque representation, with a wide, gaping mouth, but he was still tattered and dirty. I looked down at myself. I'd never let myself be seen looking that way.

I floated into the library that opened off the foyer to search for a sharp object. With careful levitating, I might maneuver it in such a way to disable the ghost from filling with air once John plugged it in. That thing was such a poor representation of what I was.

The letter opener with the cut glass handle that I had

used on a daily basis during my tenure downstairs stuck out of a porcelain jar on the desktop. It was as sharp as I remembered. I brought it to the nylon fabric protruding from the box and was about to slash the material when I had second thoughts. The children—especially the youngest ones—loved this ghost. I wouldn't spoil their fun.

I abandoned the letter opener on the large round table in the center of the foyer, next to a large orange bowl. Maggie had placed it there to hold candy for the trick or treaters.

I glanced into the living room. Eve and Roman were both sound asleep on their beds. That seemed like a good idea. We'd have a busy evening tonight. I floated up the stairs and squeezed myself through the keyhole of the attic door. I'd catch a nap and come back downstairs as soon as it began to get dark outside.

The ringing of the doorbell and barking of the dogs alerted me that things were starting downstairs. Without me. I gave myself a good shake and retraced my path to the front door at top speed.

Maggie stood in the open front door. An attractive blonde woman, who Maggie greeted as Susan, stood next to Maggie. They both smiled at John and the costumed child in front of him.

He knelt to talk to a small person dressed as a snowman. The costume had an elongated head with enormous eyes, a toothy grin, and a carrot nose. Three large, black buttons down the front completed the look. "Olaf," he said. "I'd know you anywhere."

"Yes!" The voice from inside the costume was definitely that of a little girl.

"Do you want to pick out a piece of candy?" he asked. "Grandma has the bowl."

"I've got Skittles in here," Maggie said, extending the bowl to Julia. "Your favorite."

"I'm Olaf," Julia insisted.

"So you are," Maggie said. "Would you like Skittles, Olaf?"

The large head nodded.

Maggie pulled two packages of the candy from the bowl and dropped them into the plastic pumpkin that the snowman held.

"Thank you!" Olaf said.

"I guess when she's dressed for a part, she's become that character," Susan remarked.

"I believe that's what the best actors do," Maggie replied.

"Are you looking forward to trick-or-treating, Olaf?" John addressed his granddaughter, who was the apple of his eye. He leaned close and whispered in her ear. "Maybe save a piece or two for me?"

The little girl threw her arms around his neck and hugged him. She whispered something back that I couldn't hear.

John tilted his head back and laughed.

A group of children approached up the long driveway.

"Ready to go to the next house, Olaf?" Susan reached for her hand.

The snowman nodded, and they headed down the steps.

"I'll talk to you later this week," Susan called back over her shoulder.

"I can't wait to hear all about tonight," Maggie replied.

John stood and put his arm around Maggie's shoulders.

I'd gone decades without hearing the voices of children. Rosemont had been vacant for years before Maggie had moved in. I suddenly realized how much I'd missed them.

The next group climbed the steps to the front door and hollered, "Trick or treat!" One child, dressed in a black cape and carrying a sword, jousted with the inflatable ghost as it bobbed up and down. I was doubly glad I hadn't destroyed it. I settled into a spot by the front door to enjoy the evening.

We were all tired by the time Maggie proclaimed that we'd run out of candy.

John turned out the light and unplugged the fake ghost.

Maggie picked up the empty bowl, then noticed the letter opener on the foyer table. "Did you use this for something?" She held it up to show it to John.

"No. I never use it."

"I don't either. It's more for show."

Their eyes met and held.

"It couldn't be?" Maggie asked.

John took the ornate opener from her and headed for the porcelain jar. "I think Alistair is the only explanation."

CHAPTER 9

Sunday pulled to the curb two houses down from her friend and colleague's home on Halloween. Lyla had been telling her for weeks how obsessed her husband was with his Halloween decorations. Sunday didn't want her car to block the view of Robert's spectacular offerings.

She picked up the two pizza boxes from the back seat. The tantalizing aroma from one Tomascino's meat lovers and one margherita pizza—both with extra cheese—had her mouth watering.

She'd left her post as head librarian early. It was only four-thirty now. She and Josh and Lyla and Robert would have time to eat before they settled on the porch to hand out candy. It had been years since she'd done so, and Sunday was looking forward to enjoying the evening.

She made her way past the dozen towering shapes hidden

from view by tarps to the back door leading into the kitchen. Sunday knocked lightly, then stepped inside.

"Pizza's here," she called.

Josh was the first to join her. He wore a Beast costume.

"You're dressed up," she said. "You didn't tell me."

"That's because I didn't know until about an hour ago. You've got a costume, too. Robert got them for both of us. You're Belle—being a librarian—and I'm the Beast. Just if you want to."

"Of course I do. That huge, yellow dress? How fun! It's kind of Robert. If he's gone to all that effort, I couldn't possibly say no."

"I'm glad. He's so excited. I'm seeing a whole new side of Robert."

Sunday placed her palm along his furry, costumed cheek. "You've had a blast collaborating with your dad on this Halloween extravaganza, haven't you?"

Josh nodded. "I have. There's something about working alongside someone on a big project that allows you to really get to know them."

"I'm happy for you," Sunday said. "Now—take off that mask to kiss me and eat this pizza before it gets cold. In that order."

Josh did as she directed. Lyla and Robert soon joined them. Lyla took Sunday to the spare bedroom after they finished eating the last slice of pizza.

Sunday transformed herself into Belle. "This costume is beautiful." She ran her hands over the fitted bodice and executed a pirouette to test the long, full skirt.

Lyla chuckled.

"I loved twirling in my Disney princess costumes when I was a kid," Sunday said sheepishly.

"I'm happy you're enjoying your costume," Lyla said. She transformed herself into Dorothy, complete with a stuffed Toto, to go with Robert's cowardly lion.

The four costumed adults took their seats on the front porch as the first trick-or-treaters arrived.

They were busy handing out candy when an Elsa and an Olaf met on the sidewalk. They were both accompanied by a parent.

"Susan!" The little girl in the Elsa costume threw her arms around the mother of the other child. "Julia is Olaf? That's perfect for us to trick-or-treat together."

"Hi, Nicole. You look beautiful. Elsa's blue dress is the perfect color for you." Susan hugged her much younger half-sister before bending over to address her own three-year-old. "Julia, would you like to go up to the door with Nicole?"

Olaf's head bobbed up and down.

"Good." Susan stood.

Nicole held out her hand to Julia, and the toddler took it. Together, they mounted the steps to the porch, bypassing the maze.

Susan turned to Frank Haynes. "Where are Sean and Marissa?"

"They're too big to want to trick-or-treat with their dad. It took some convincing, but Loretta finally allowed them to go out as long as they stick together. They have to check in by phone every thirty minutes and be home by nine."

Susan and Frank sauntered up to the door behind Elsa and Olaf. "I'm glad we ran into you. Julia was excited to put her costume on and go out tonight. We started at Rosemont, and she loved it, but she's balked at every house we've come to since."

"I guess going to your grandparents' house seems familiar," Frank commented.

"That must be it. Julia loves candy and we rarely let her have any, so I keep reminding her that people are giving out all her favorites. Even that doesn't entice her. We stand at the curb and watch as other children race up to front doors, fill their buckets, and tear off to the next house."

Nicole walked onto the porch to the four adults sitting in lawn chairs by the door. "Trick-or-treat," she yelled.

Julia took a step back.

Nicole kept hold of her hand, pulling her forward. "Say it. Or you won't get candy."

Julia hesitated, then the familiar words escaped her lips in a whisper.

Lyla leaned forward and offered the candy bowl. "My goodness—don't the two of you look perfect together? Elsa and Olaf, right?"

Nicole nodded as she selected a packet of gummy worms and encouraged Julia to take a piece of candy. "Just one," she told the little girl.

Julia pulled out a fruit roll-up.

"How polite. You can take another piece—if it's all right with your parents?" Lyla looked at Frank and Susan.

"Thank you," Susan said. "It's okay, Julia."

Frank nodded his agreement.

The girls helped themselves again. This time, Julia needed no encouragement.

"I think she may be getting the hang of it," Frank said to Susan.

"Thank you," Nicole said to Lyla. "You have to say that, too," she told Julia.

The little girl's voice was louder as she thanked Lyla.

"If you have older kids, they'll want to stop by after eight," Josh said. "See all those tarps?" He gestured to the shrouded shapes along both sides of the house and down the driveway. "Those will come off and it'll be *real* spooky."

"I wondered what was under all that," Susan commented. "You've gone all out."

"These two sure have," Sunday said, pointing to Josh and Robert. "I got a glimpse of what's under those tarps last weekend and it's terrifying."

"I have a middle schooler and one in high school," Frank said. "I'll tell them about it and drive them over. They'll want to experience this."

"Can we go through the maze?" Nicole asked. "Or is that for big kids only, too?"

"The maze will be perfect for you," Robert said. "Let me show you." He walked them to the row of hay bales snaking across the yard.

Nicole stepped into the maze. "I see a friendly ghost!" she hollered. "Come on, Julia."

Elsa and Olaf entered the short maze and soon came out the other end, their clasped hands swinging together.

"Do you mind if we tag along with you and Nicole?" Susan asked Frank.

"I don't think we could separate them if we tried," Frank said. "And I'd be happy for the company."

They followed their children to the next house, and this time Olaf pulled ahead of Elsa.

CHAPTER 10

Maggie parked in her reserved spot behind the Highpointe College Administration Building and got out of her car. Even from the rear edifice, the red brick structure was a stunning example of collegiate gothic architecture. The structure had kept watch over the campus for almost one hundred seventy-five years. She wondered if any of her twenty predecessors—she was the twenty-first president of Highpointe—had stopped where she stood now, drawing strength from its majesty before entering the office she occupied.

One of the double doors to the suite marked Office of the President in gleaming brass letters stood open. It was shortly before nine on the morning after Halloween, and she'd told Josh he could be late coming in. She didn't have any meetings or conference calls on her schedule. The day would consist of her reviewing financial reports. Maggie could manage without her administrative assistant being at his post outside her door for an hour.

The dependable Josh was at his desk anyway. He looked up at her as she stepped into the reception area, the phone to his ear. He put his hand over the receiver. "It's Gordon Mortimer," he said quietly. "Would you like me to take a message?"

Maggie shook her head no and hurried into her office. She slung her purse onto her desk and dropped her satchel on the floor. The phone on her desk rang with the transferred call, and she picked it up while sliding into her chair.

"Gordon," Maggie said. "I'm so happy to hear from you."

"Thank you, madam."

The corners of Maggie's lips turned up at the customary formality of the antiques appraiser from New York City whom she and John now thought of as a close friend. "Please—Gordon—you've got to call me Maggie."

"Sorry, madam. Maggie. Old habits die hard."

"I hope you're calling to tell me that we'll see you in person soon."

"You will, indeed. That is, if it's convenient for you. It's rather short notice, but I've had an unexpected cancellation. I'm available two weeks from Sunday. I plan to stay the entire week."

"That's perfect," Maggie replied quickly. "I was afraid we wouldn't see you until after the New Year."

"If it hadn't been for this cancellation, that's what would have happened."

"You'll stay with us, at Rosemont, of course." Maggie extended the invitation as if it had already been accepted.

"If it wouldn't be too much trouble. I'll leave the Sunday before Thanksgiving. I remember you host a large gathering that day, so you may not want a house guest underfoot while you prepare for that."

"Nonsense. You've stayed with us before, and you are the most congenial house guest imaginable."

"That's kind of you, mad … Maggie," Gordon corrected himself.

"Getting ready for Thanksgiving isn't a big deal. It's a potluck, so that makes it easy for me. All I have to do is set the table—or tables, since we usually host at least thirty."

"My goodness—that's a sizable crowd."

"It's so much fun. Everyone brings a show-off dish to share. After dinner, we all go outside to ooh and ahh over John's Christmas light display. He's working on it like mad right now and turns it on for the first time at dusk on Thanksgiving."

Maggie relaxed against the back of her chair as she basked in memories of the day that meant so much to her now that she'd settled into Rosemont. "Marc Benson is a professional musician and leads us in a Christmas-carol sing-along by the piano in the conservatory. A large group plays Pictionary. By then, everyone is ready for a second helping of dessert."

"It sounds …" Gordon's voice cracked, and he paused to regain control of his emotions. "Like something out of a movie."

"Why don't you extend your visit and stay another week? Be with us for Thanksgiving. I know you'd enjoy it—you've already met most of the people who will be attending. John and I would love to have you."

"That's most generous of you." Gordon cleared his throat. "I simply can't. I have engagements in my diary that week that require my presence here."

"I'm sorry to hear that," Maggie said, and her voice echoed her disappointment. "It's a standing offer, however. If things change, we'd love to have you."

"Thank you."

"We'll see you in time for dinner on the day you arrive?"

"You don't need to worry about feeding me."

"I'd love to make you a home-cooked meal. Sunday is the only day I can reliably turn out a good dinner since I'm so busy at the college. I enjoy cooking for John and myself every Sunday. Adding one more is no big deal."

"Once again, thank you."

"I'll board Blossom, Buttercup, and Bubbles at Westbury Animal Hospital while you're with us, too. I recall how allergic you are to cats."

"You're kind to remember, and I'm grateful."

"I can't wait to learn what other treasures are in Rosemont's attic," Maggie said.

"That makes two of us."

"We'll see you soon, then."

"Before we go, can I ask a favor?"

"Of course, Gordon. What do you need?"

"Would you send me Anita Archer's contact information?

I'd like to set up a time to view her collection of vintage sewing machines."

"I'll email it to you as soon as we hang up." Maggie smiled. "I ran into Anita last week. She's excited to show you her collection."

"I'm interested in seeing it. There's one thing, though." He paused before he continued. "I've checked around. The vintage sewing machine market isn't strong at the moment. Especially for ones that have been heavily used."

"Anita's machines were part of the wedding dress alteration business she took over from her grandmother. I'm sure they're well worn."

"I'm afraid she'll be disappointed if she hopes to sell them for a significant amount."

"She's never talked about them like they're her retirement nest egg."

"I'm relieved to hear it. And I meant it when I said I'm looking forward to seeing them. Even utilitarian objects from that era were beautifully made and graciously adorned."

Maggie grinned. "You are a connoisseur with wide-ranging interests, Gordon."

"That's a wonderful compliment, madam."

"Maggie," she said in exasperation. "Take care, Gordon. John and I look forward to seeing you soon."

CHAPTER 11

Maggie closed out of the financial statements she'd been reviewing online all morning. The college was on firm financial footing. Alumni donations exceeded projections, despite the negative publicity from the recently uncovered theft of rare books from Highpointe's collection.

The books had been stolen decades earlier and their loss discovered by Sunday Sloan—their charismatic rare book librarian. The salacious fact that the thief had tried to kill Sunday—in the college library, after hours—had landed the story on the front page of newspapers all over the country. Maggie raised her hands above her head and stretched. What was the old saying? There's no such thing as bad publicity? Thank God her attacker hadn't succeeded, Maggie thought.

She glanced out the bank of windows behind her. The sun shone in a cloudless, azure sky. Trees lining the quadrangle were thick with leaves in every shade from gold to orange to deep crimson. This might be the last fine day of the season. Fall would bow out of the picture in Westbury soon, making way for the icy winds and gray skies of winter. Maggie picked up her purse and left her office. She'd head to Celebrations to complete her wedding gift for Pam and Steve, then stroll along the square to pick up lunch from Pete's Bistro.

Josh sat at his desk, hunched over a sheaf of papers spread out in front of him.

"You're not working through lunch, are you?" Maggie didn't approve of people eating at their desks—even though she did so regularly. She believed that taking a midday break made one more productive in the afternoon.

He glanced up at her. "I'm working on a proposal for a project. It's required for one of my classes."

Maggie stopped in front of his desk and nodded encouragingly.

"I'm interested in philanthropic partnerships," he said. "The way in which charities and other institutions—like schools, colleges, or communities—can work together in simple ways to benefit each other."

"I like the sound of that," Maggie said. "Tell me more."

"You know my pup, Dan, was a rescue?"

"I remember."

"I can't dismiss the thought that he came close to being put to sleep." He dropped his pen onto his papers. "It's unbelievable no one wanted the sweetest black Lab in the world."

"People must not have known he was at the shelter. If

we'd have seen him, I'm sure John and I would have brought him home."

"Exactly!" Josh rested his elbows on his desk and leaned forward. "These dogs need to get out into the community. They need to be seen."

"Instead of waiting for people to walk into the shelter."

"Yep. I've been researching ways to increase shelter adoption rates. Based on the numbers I've seen from similar programs, I'd like to propose a program where people can take a dog out of a shelter for a day on the town. They can walk them in the park, along the square, or take them to the farmers market. It doesn't matter where they go, as long as other people see them."

"What an interesting idea," Maggie said.

"You could go to the shelter's website and sign up to be paired with the animal you choose. The shelter would have already posted detailed information about the dog's age, energy level, and demeanor online. You'd pick up the dog in the morning and return it in the afternoon. The dog would wear a vest with the words 'I'm looking for my forever home' and the name and phone number of the shelter. People would be expected to take the dog out in public."

"This works?"

"Seven out of ten dogs taken out for a day like this are adopted that day."

"By the person who took them out?"

"Sometimes, but, generally, no. Most are placed with people who came across them while the dog was out and about."

"Proving that out of sight, out of mind, is the rule for shelter dogs."

"Exactly."

"Sounds like a worthy project." Maggie leaned across the desk to peer at his papers. "What are you thinking?"

"I'd like to pitch the idea to our local shelter here in Westbury—Forever Friends. I'd set up the program and keep records on it for a report I'd turn in at the end of the semester."

"I'm sure Frank Haynes will love this idea."

"You are?"

"Without a doubt."

"The shelter staff will have to be available to release the dogs that have been selected and intake them when they're returned. That makes more work for them. Do you think he'll object to that?"

"Not in a million years. Frank started the shelter years ago because he is an animal softie. He'll be happy that they get a day out and thrilled if they find homes."

"I understand he's a very busy man ..."

"And you've heard he can be very gruff? That he's a hard-hearted business executive?"

Josh nodded. "That's his reputation about town. Although I met him last night when he brought his kids to trick-or-treat at Robert and Lyla's. He stopped by twice, as a matter of fact. He seemed really nice."

"When I first moved to Westbury, Frank and I were enemies." Maggie pursed her lips and shook her head at the memory. "Now? I consider him a kind and devoted family man. And a friend. I'd love to do an email introduction of the two of you."

"That would be super helpful."

"You'll find him very receptive," Maggie said. "I'll do it as soon as I get back. I'm headed to the square to run an errand and I'm stopping at Pete's to grab lunch to go." She smiled at her assistant. She'd miss him when he graduated and moved on. "I'll bring back lunch for you, too."

"You don't have to …"

"I want to," Maggie said, moving to the door. "Text me what you want from Pete's and I'll be back here in ninety minutes."

CHAPTER 12

A parking spot on the far side of the square from Celebrations opened up and Maggie slid her car into it. Walking across the square was one of her favorite things to do in Westbury. It was close enough to Rosemont to be one of Roman and Eve's regular outings. She'd have to remember to bring them here on the upcoming weekend if the weather was clear.

She tucked the silver pitcher, wrapped in a tea towel, under her arm and set out. The canopy of flaming-hued leaves from the towering trees on the square created a thick carpet of shade on the wide cement pathways. Squirrels raced across the lawn and up the thick trunks, acorns bulging in their mouths.

Maggie stopped to watch one ambitious fellow all the way to his nest high in the treetop, until he was eventually camouflaged by the bark. She stood, breathing in the crisp air and soaking in the beauty on every side.

Her thoughts turned to Vermont as she remembered the glorious vistas of fall trees there. At least they *were* glorious, she thought, until a forest fire destroyed them. Maggie said a silent prayer for the people who had lost homes, businesses, and more.

She stepped out from under the canopy of trees and onto the sidewalk. As she looked back at the square, she thought about how heartbroken she would be if it had been destroyed. All the more reason to do something nice for the young couple in Linden Falls, she thought.

She crossed the street and headed down the long block toward Celebrations. The sun warmed her shoulders through her navy blazer, making her uncomfortably hot. While she was removing the blazer, the door to the shop opened and Anita Archer stepped out.

Maggie waved, but her friend had her back to her and hurried away in the opposite direction.

Maggie stepped into Celebrations to find it deserted except for its proprietor, Judy Young, who was restocking a display of knitted winter scarves.

"Hi, Maggie." Judy abandoned her task and turned her attention to the woman who had become one of her best customers over the years.

Maggie walked over to Judy and lightly fingered one of the scarves. "These are lovely."

"Thank you. They're new this year. I just put them out last week and thought I'd made a mistake bringing them into the store because I hadn't sold one of them—until this morning. By lunchtime, I'd sold a half dozen. Did you see Anita leaving here?"

Maggie nodded.

"She bought one. Said they're made from the finest alpaca yarn she's seen in years."

"Anita would know. That's quite a compliment." Maggie extricated a scarf in shades of taupe and blush pink from the display. "Susan would love this. I'll put it away for her Christmas present."

Judy took the scarf from her. "Smart. That's the only one I received in those colors. They're all handmade." She moved to the register. "Did you come in for anything else?" She eyed the bumpy parcel tucked under Maggie's arm.

Maggie told Judy what she had in mind while she unwrapped the pitcher.

Judy nodded in appreciation. "That's a stunning piece. It sounds like you've found someone who will appreciate it and give it a perfect home."

"If it wasn't a wedding present, I'd send one of those scarves. A scarf would be odd, being only for one person."

Judy's eyes twinkled. "I've got just the thing." She took the pitcher from Maggie and set it behind the register with the scarf. "Follow me."

Judy led her to a decorative ladder leaning against the back wall. It had a variety of throws and blankets folded across its rungs. Judy pulled a throw in muted shades of cream, taupe, and blush from the rack.

"That looks a bit like the scarf I'm buying."

Judy nodded. "It's made by the same artisan. They added cream to the color palette. I ordered four throws, but this is the only one that came in."

Maggie lifted the delicate fabric. "It's so lightweight."

"Yes—but it's very strong. And warm. That's what the artisan said and Anita confirmed it."

"I haven't known Pam for long, but we got close while we were working with those poor animals. She and Steve were the kindest people."

"I heard about what you and John did," Judy said. "You made Westbury proud."

"My gut tells me she'll love it." Maggie looked at the price tag and took a step back.

"Don't you worry about the cost," Judy said. "You can have it at half off."

Maggie looked at her friend. "No way—you won't make a dime on it."

"I don't need to make money on everything, Maggie. If this couple is as nice as you say they are, I want them to have it."

Maggie stared at her.

"Let me do this for you, Maggie."

"If you insist."

"I do."

"That's very nice of you. I can't wait for them to get this. I wish I could be a fly on the wall when they open it."

"Me, too," Judy said. "If things don't get too busy, I can pack the pitcher and throw and send them out this afternoon."

"I need to pick out a wedding card," Maggie said, heading for the racks of cards.

"You do that, and I'll gift wrap everything."

Maggie picked out an elegant card with a simple inscription, wrote a personal note of congratulations, and took it to the register.

Judy tied the final loop of an elaborate white bow in iridescent ribbon. She placed the card with the package. "Let me ring you up."

Maggie handed Judy her credit card to process the transaction.

"It'll be fun to see Gordon again soon," Judy said.

Maggie's head snapped up. "How do you know about his visit?"

"Anita told me. That's why she stopped in. She's very excited about it."

"I sent Anita's email address to Gordon not more than three hours ago," Maggie said.

"He contacted her, she responded, they talked, and they've scheduled an appointment."

"Wow. News travels fast in Westbury. It shouldn't surprise me after all these years, but it always does."

"Especially if it's good news," Judy agreed. "We love good news around here."

Maggie stuffed the credit card receipt in her purse. "I'd better get going. I need to stop at Pete's to pick up lunch to take back to my office."

"I'm glad you came in." Judy stepped around the counter and hugged her customer.

"I'm hosting the Thanksgiving potluck at Rosemont again this year. Can you and Jeff make it?"

"We wouldn't miss it for the world," Judy said. "That brings up another thing—something as a retail shopkeeper I never thought I'd do."

Maggie held her friend at arm's length. "What's that?"

"Jeff is working his fingers to the bone to finish restoring the Olsson House by Christmas. His kids and grandkids are coming for the holiday. He'd like to hold an open house on Christmas afternoon."

"What a fabulous idea! You should do that. Everyone is dying to see what you've done to the place."

"I don't want to compete with your Rosemont Christmas party." Judy drew the words out until they sounded like a question.

"Don't be silly. We don't own Christmas, for heaven's sake. Do you plan to invite the same people we do?"

Judy nodded.

"Then let's hold Christmas at your house. We'll announce it at Thanksgiving."

"You don't mind?"

"Not at all," Maggie said. "And if you want a hand with anything—or need extra chairs or serving pieces—say the word. You already know what I have at Rosemont. You're welcome to borrow any of it."

Judy drew Maggie back in for a tight hug. "You're a wonderful friend, Maggie Martin."

CHAPTER 13

The receptionist at Forever Friends hung up the phone and smiled at Josh. "Mr. Haynes will be right out."

Josh nodded and stepped close to a large flat-screen television affixed to a wall. Images of dogs and cats scrolled across the screen. A stationary banner at the bottom announced that all the animals were available to become someone's forever friend. He stared into the yearning eyes of a small German shepherd and wondered if Dan needed another dog to keep him company. The image was soon replaced with the photo of a long-haired cat. He stood, transfixed to the screen, waiting for the German shepherd to come back, when he heard his name being called.

Josh turned as the tall, lanky man he remembered from Halloween approached him with an outstretched hand. "Josh Newlon?"

Josh nodded and shook Frank's hand.

"Thank you for agreeing to see me, Mr. Haynes."

"Frank—please. Let's go to my office. Have you ever been here before?"

Josh fell in line with Frank. "I haven't."

"Let me give you a quick tour on the way," Frank veered off to his left. He showed Josh the animal intake area, dog and cat washing areas, an employee break room that also housed medical supplies, and finally took them up and down the rows of kennels. Frank spoke to each dog or cat by name. Even the ones that huddled in the back of their kennel came up to Frank for a kind word and an ear rub through the metal grates.

Josh followed behind, pausing in front of the German shepherd's kennel. The card posted on the outside said the dog was a female, probably two years old, and was good with other large dogs. The dog paced in front of him, keeping her eyes glued to his. Josh stuck his hand through the grate, and she walked over to allow him to run a finger along her muzzle. "Good girl," Josh cooed.

The dog swept her tongue over his hand.

"She's a grand dog," Frank said. "We've got three dogs and five kids at home—including infant twins—or I'd adopt her myself. I asked my wife about it, and she said she'd kill me with her bare hands if I even mentioned it again."

Josh laughed. "I can understand why she feels that way."

"Do you have a pet?"

"An enormous black Lab. Dan was a rescue, just like these guys."

The dog pressed herself against the front of her kennel and Josh moved on to rubbing her ears.

"Does Dan need a ... companion?"

Josh pulled his hand back. "I'm in an apartment. One big dog is more than enough there."

Frank ran his eyes from Josh, to the dog, and back again. "I assume you walk Dan?"

"Every day. He gets plenty of exercise."

"Walking two dogs doesn't take more time than walking one," Frank said.

Josh raised a hand in protest.

"I don't want to put you on the spot," Frank interjected quickly. "There just seems to be a connection between the two of you. You can always think about it. You said in your email you have a proposal for me?"

"Yes."

Frank pointed to a door at the end of the corridor. "That's my office. Would you like a cup of coffee before we get started?"

"I'm fine, but thank you."

Frank ushered them into his office and pointed to one of two chairs sitting in front of his desk.

Josh sat, and Frank lowered himself into the other chair.

"I'm working on a master's degree in college administration," Josh said. "The project I'm proposing to you is in connection with a class on collaborative community projects."

"I'm expanding this facility into a guide dog training school to be named Forever Guides, but we haven't broken ground yet. I don't see how Forever Friends has anything to do with higher education."

"This project has nothing to do with education—yet. I've got ideas on that. But, to begin, it would simply be a collaboration between the shelter and members of the community."

Frank nodded, signaling him to continue.

Josh explained the program that had achieved a 70 percent adoption rate for dogs taken out of shelters for a day.

"That's impressive. And they're not all taken by the people who enroll in the program?"

"That's right."

Frank raised an eyebrow.

"I'm surprised by this finding, too. Traffic into shelters increased significantly on days when dogs were enjoying days out. Exposure is the key driver of this result."

Josh removed a thin three-ring binder from his satchel. He turned to a page that contained color photos of vests in a variety of sizes. "We'd need the dogs to wear vests like these when they're out and about. I mocked up three designs for a Doggie Day Out logo for you to consider." He turned to the next page and handed the binder to Frank.

"These are all good," Frank said. "Do you have a background in graphic design?"

"No. I paint, so maybe that gives me ideas about form and the use of colors."

"There's no 'maybe' about it. You're good." He pointed to a logo that depicted an outline of a large dog walking at the end of a leash with the letters DDO in the middle. "I'd like to try your program. Let's use this logo."

"That's fantastic," Josh said. "You're going to be very happy with the results. I'll stay involved and help every step of the way."

"I appreciate that. Our staff is stretched to the limits as it is."

"I know how busy you are running Haynes Enterprises and this shelter—plus expanding into a guide dog training school."

"I've hired Neil Parker as my new chief operating officer of Haynes Enterprises. That helps a lot."

"He's married to Sherry, the new vet at Westbury Animal Hospital. I took Dan to see her for his recent checkup."

"That's right. Sherry's been a big help already with the guide dog school. She interned at one of the large schools on the East Coast."

"I was surprised you even found time to see me today," Josh said.

"Forever Friends is a no-kill shelter," Frank said. "I'm always interested in ways to improve adoption rates so we don't become overcrowded. I heard about a program within the California prison system where they take shelter dogs into prisons and allow inmates to train them as service dogs for military veterans with PTSD. It's good for the dogs, the veterans who need them, and it rehabilitates inmates. With everything I've got on my plate right now, I haven't had time to contact anyone to start a similar program in our state."

"That sounds like a worthy cause."

"I'm not giving up on it. In the meantime, your idea could help a lot of animals find their forever homes right here and now." Frank tossed the binder onto this desktop and stood. "Maybe you can be the first participant." Frank looked at Josh and his eyes twinkled. "You can take that sweet girl who caught your eye on the way into my office for a doggie day out."

Josh got to his feet. "Or maybe I could stay a while longer and take her into a get-acquainted room?"

Frank clapped Josh on the back. "I like the sound of that. You most certainly can." He opened a desk drawer and grabbed a ring of keys. "I'll get the two of you set up myself."

Frank glanced out his office window thirty minutes later. A smile as wide as a jack-o-lantern's split his face. Josh was headed to the parking lot, the German shepherd trotting at his side.

CHAPTER 14

"Something smells good!" Steve Turner came through the back door and crossed to the stove to kiss his bride.

His dog, Chance, rubbed against their legs, pacing, until they pulled apart and Steve reached down to pet him. "Hey, buddy. Don't be jealous. You need to get used to this." He gestured between himself and Pam. "We're married now."

The black Lab mix uttered a single "Woof."

Pam got down on one knee and ran her hands up and down on either side of his neck. "We're a family now. You, Steve, me—and Leopold." She looked at her cat, perched in his favorite spot on top of an old-fashioned pine hutch, his tail twitching where it draped over the side.

The cat looked away at the same time as Chance did.

"It may take more time to make us into a happy, blended

family," Steve said. He stood and pulled her to her feet. "What're you making?"

"Spaghetti and meatballs," Pam replied. "Don't get too excited. The meatballs came from the freezer and the sauce is from a jar. I spruced it up with some fresh herbs, and there's garlic bread in the oven, but that's the best I can muster after working all day."

"You're a wonderful cook and I'm not complaining. But we can go out or order in every night as far as I'm concerned. That's what I did before we got married."

She stood on her tiptoes and kissed his cheek.

"Are we ready to eat?"

"In a minute. My last two clients of the day canceled, so I had time to pick up that mysterious package Paige was holding for us before I came home."

"Did you open it?"

Pam shook her head, snatched a pair of scissors from a jar on the kitchen counter, and beckoned him to follow her into the foyer. A medium-sized, rectangular parcel, wrapped in brown butcher paper, sat on the console table.

"It was all I could do to stay out of it," she said. "It's from Maggie Martin and John Allen."

"The vet and his nice wife?"

Pam nodded. "Paige told me it's a wedding present."

"You're kidding me."

"Maggie stopped in Paige's store before they went back home to verify that Paige is our postmistress. She said she'd heard about our wedding the following weekend and wanted to send us a gift but didn't have our address. Paige told her to send the package to her store, and she'd get it to us."

"Now I'm curious to see what it is."

Pam snipped the twine wrapped around the parcel. "There's more. Maggie asked Paige if she knew us—she was trying to figure out what we like. Paige told her I'd bought and restored my grandmother's old house, and that we moved in here after we got married. She said this place is full of antiques." Pam began snipping at the copious amounts of tape on the package.

"Can I help?" Steve took the scissors from her and used them like a knife, slicing through the tape.

"Paige said Maggie practically squealed. Turns out she and John live in some historic mansion known as Rosemont. It has an attic full of valuable antiques, including vintage and hotel silver. Maggie told Paige she'd send us a piece from the collection in her attic."

"Now I'm really impressed that you haven't already opened this. You adore that stuff." He ripped the butcher paper away, revealing a beautifully wrapped gift.

Pam opened the card and read aloud. "John and I loved meeting you and speak about you often. Our time together was short, but we bonded deeply during the wildfire crisis. The pitcher is from my attic. I want you to have something personal from us. The throw is for you to cuddle up in during the cold Vermont winters. May you have a long and joyful life together. Much love, Maggie & John."

She pressed the card to her chest. "Aww ... that's so nice." She set it on the table. "Do you want to open it?"

"No way." He held the wrapped package out to her.

Pam tore away the gift wrap and opened the box. She reached in and carefully separated the pitcher from the throw that Judy had used to protect the pitcher.

"Holy cow," Steve said as Pam held the pitcher up to the light of the overhead pendant.

Pam gasped. "This is absolutely stunning." She rested its graceful feet on her palm and turned it this way and that. "Look at the lines of this piece. The proportions."

"What do we do with it?"

"I'm going to display it," Pam said. "In my grandmother's hutch in the dining room. I wish she were still alive to see this. She'd have loved it."

Steve squinted as he peered at the underside. "There's a mark on it."

Pam turned it over and gasped again. "It's not silver plate." She turned wide eyes to his. "This is solid sterling. I'm going to keep this polished and displayed for the rest of my life."

She scooped the throw out of the box. "And look at this! It'll be perfect at the end of our bed. The colors fit right in with our bedroom."

"I can picture you curled up for naps in that," Steve said.

"Let's put this where it belongs," she held up the pitcher, "and go eat. I'll write a thank you note after dinner."

CHAPTER 15

Pam placed her knife and fork across her plate and pushed back her chair. She reached for her plate, but Steve put out a hand to stop her.

"You did all the cooking; I'll clear the table and clean up the kitchen."

"Thank you. I want to email the two clients who haven't already canceled their training appointments during the week of Thanksgiving. They're diehards and will be disappointed, but we need to take our honeymoon."

"Absolutely. Everyone needs a break from time to time—including self-employed personal trainers." He took their plates to the sink and opened the dishwasher.

"I want to get away. A staycation isn't what I have in mind," Pam said.

"I agree. And if people see us around town, they won't understand why we canceled their sessions."

"Exactly. Now we have to figure out where to go."

"Leaf-peeping season will be over, so we'll find vacancies at most of the charming inns all over New England. Or we can head to the Caribbean for a beach vacay." He rinsed the remains of the pasta sauce from a sauté pan and placed it in the dishwasher. "We can do whatever we want."

Chance circled at their feet. Steve usually threw him a leftover morsel rather than dispense with it in the garbage disposal. He was not to be disappointed tonight: Steve sent the last remaining meatball in a high arc. Chance leapt and snagged it on the way down, swallowing it before his paws hit the floor.

"I can't do it," Pam blurted out, her voice wavering with emotion.

Steve put the pasta water pot in the sink and turned to her. "Can't do what?"

"Leave Chance behind. With a dog sitter." Her chin quivered.

"Carol and her family have offered to take him. Chance'll be fine."

A tear slid down her cheek. "He got lost during the fire and—for all we know—almost died. I can't stand the thought of leaving him—not so soon after we got him back."

Steve turned off the water and moved to her, encircling her with his arms. "I didn't know you felt this way."

"I'm sorry. I don't want to ruin our honeymoon." Her voice was muffled against his shirt. "We need to bring him with us and we'll have to stay close to home because I can't stand the thought of Chance traveling in the cargo hold of a plane."

"You're not ruining anything. I won't allow him to travel that way, either." He paused, thinking through the ramifications of this decision. "We'll be driving rather than flying, so maybe New England is a good choice. If we can't find an inn that will allow a hundred-pound dog, I'm sure we can find a vacation rental online."

She tilted her head back. "You don't mind bringing Chance with us on our honeymoon?"

Steve smiled into her tear-rimmed eyes. "To be honest, I'd feel better if he was with us. I guess we're both a couple of softies."

Chance thumped his tail against the floor and emitted a sharp bark.

"I think he's telling us to hurry," Steve said. "He wants his after-dinner walk."

Pam glanced at the clock on the wall. "It's that time."

"I'll finish up here in a few minutes and then we can go."

"Do you mind if I stay home tonight? I'll email my clients and begin looking for vacation rentals. We've only got three weeks to find a place."

"Sure."

Pam knelt and stroked Chance along his back. "You're coming with us, sweet boy. Leopold will go to my mom's—he loves staying at his grandma's—but you'll be with us."

Chance barked again.

"I swear he understands us," Steve said. He hung the dish

towel on its hook and started the dishwasher as Pam took her laptop into the living room.

Chance pranced to the kitchen door and twirled in circles until Steve snapped his leash onto his collar and they set out into the crisp night.

∽

Steve and Chance returned from their walk an hour later. The big dog raced through the house, looking for Pam. He found her on the sofa. She had changed into her faded flannel pajamas and wrapped herself in the new alpaca throw. Her feet were on the coffee table, her laptop balanced on her thighs.

Chance flung himself onto the sofa next to her, wriggling with excitement.

Pam reached out a hand to calm him. "What's gotten into him?" She asked Steve as he entered the room.

"You'll never guess what we ran into on our walk."

Pam raised a quizzical eyebrow.

"A skunk. Rummaging in the trash cans of a house two streets over."

Alarmed, Pam pulled her hand away and put her other hand to her head and groaned. "At least he didn't get sprayed, right?"

"He took one look at that skunk and took off in the other direction. I swear—we ran at least a half mile."

"Good boy!" Pam planted a kiss on the top of Chance's

head. "You remembered your earlier unfortunate incident with a skunk."

"He did indeed."

"You're very smart, Chance. I've been so engrossed in what I've been doing" —Pam looked up at Steve as she tapped her laptop— "that I hadn't noticed how long you've been gone."

"He was fired up, so we kept walking. I wanted to calm him down. I'm sorry I'm so late getting back."

"No worries. I think I've found where we should go for our honeymoon." She moved Chance off the sofa and beckoned for Steve to sit next to her. "Let me show you."

Steve sank down next to her.

She angled the screen of her laptop to him. "What do you think of this vacation rental?"

Steve scrolled through the photos of an A-frame house constructed of cedar planks with a massive stone fireplace on one end and a wall of windows on the other. An elevated redwood deck surrounded the home. Interior photos captured a spectacular wooded view through the floor-to-ceiling windows. A primary bedroom was furnished with a king-sized bed sporting an ornately carved headboard and made up with a deep white duvet. The en suite bath contained a soaker tub and a generous shower with the latest fittings.

"The decor is all rich, jewel-tone rugs, white linens, and comfy, leather seating. Very Ralph Lauren," Pam said.

"Other than his polo shirts, I don't know much about the guy. Except you like his style." He read the written description of the property. "It's new construction, decorated to look old. That sounds good. It says it backs up to a state park full of hiking and biking trails and is only a short drive from Westbury. I've never heard of it. Where is this?"

"Westbury is where John and Maggie live."

"That's quite a way from us." He looked puzzled. "Why did you find a place there?"

"Paige told me about Rosemont. She found it on the internet and says it's fabulous. That's the name of Maggie and John's house—where the silver pitcher was in the attic." Pam looked at Steve. "We'd appreciate our gift so much more if we saw where it came from."

"So, you found it online?"

"Yep. Wait until I show you—I kept the tab open. It's the most amazing house."

"How did Rosemont lead to this fabulous vacation rental?"

"You know how internet research goes. It's like you disappear down one rabbit hole into another. I looked at the college where Maggie works, then I found John's animal hospital, which is near the most charming town square you've ever seen. Before long, I knew all about the place. And I found this." She pointed to her laptop screen. "The most perfect place for our honeymoon."

"How long a drive is it?"

"Two days. We can sightsee along the way. It'll be too cold to camp, but there are plenty of dog-friendly hotels on our route. We'd only need to spend one night each way."

He scrolled through the photos again. "It sure suits us," he said. "We can hike, we can explore the area, or we can hole up and ignore the world."

"That's what I thought." She turned bright eyes to him. "So—you like it?"

He nodded.

"Shall I book it?"

"You'd better. We don't want it to get away."

Pam squealed and clicked on the button to secure their reservation.

"I love the idea of a week far away from here, where we have no set plans and no deadlines," Steve said.

"Me, too," Pam replied. She paused, her fingers hovering over her keyboard. "There's only one thing I want to do for sure."

He cocked an eyebrow at her. "Let me guess." A smile slid from ear to ear. "You want to drive by Rosemont."

Pam grinned. "You know me so well."

"Then driving by Rosemont will be on our list."

Pam resumed filling out the form, entered their credit card number, and hit submit.

Steve shut her laptop and placed it on the coffee table.

"Don't you want to see Rosemont?" Pam asked.

"I can wait." Steve stood and pulled her to her feet before leading them to the bedroom.

CHAPTER 16

Sunday abandoned the box of rare books she was cataloging and dove for her cell phone. Josh was calling. She swiped to answer the call seconds before it would have gone to voicemail.

"Hi," she said, slightly out of breath.

"Did I catch you at a bad time?"

Sunday put her hand on her hip and stretched backward. "Not at all. I've been hunched over a box of books all morning. So glad you called. I need a break."

"Good. I won't keep you. Can you come to dinner at my place tonight? I'm celebrating."

"Did Frank say yes to your doggie day out program?"

"Yes. I just got done talking to him. I'd love to tell you all about it."

"And I'd love to hear it. Since we're celebrating, I'll take you out to dinner. Where would you like to go?"

"No. I mean—thank you, but no. I'd like you to come to my place. I've got steaks. This may be my last chance to use my grill before winter hits. And I've got someone I want you to meet."

"All right. I'll bring dessert. Laura's will be closed by the time I get off of work, but I'll swing by Pete's and pick up three pieces of apple pie to go."

"They don't eat pie. You'll only need two pieces."

"Won't that be rude to eat pie in front of them? I'll run to the grocery for something else. What do you think they'd like?"

"Don't worry about it," Josh said. "Come over after work. I've got to go. Can't wait to see you." He ended the call without waiting for her reply.

Sunday returned to her task, replaying the call over and over in her mind. There was something Josh wasn't telling her.

She was unlocking her car after picking up three pieces of apple pie from Pete's—an extra piece of pie would never go to waste around Josh—when a thought hit her. Sunday chuckled as she got behind the wheel. She had an extra errand to add to her itinerary before she arrived at Josh's house for dinner.

∽

Sunday knocked on Josh's door twenty minutes later. Dan's familiar, low, throaty bark sounded immediately. There was another sound with it—coming from further back in the apartment. It was a full-bodied bark—not a high-pitched yipping—but Dan was definitely not making this noise.

The latch clicked, and Sunday forced the smile from her face as Josh opened the door. She didn't want to spoil his surprise. At least not yet.

Josh ushered her in and took the takeout box bearing the Pete's Bistro logo from her and set it on the counter.

As they always did after they'd been apart for even a day or two, they fell into each other's arms and kissed.

Dan stood next to them, silently wagging his tail, waiting for the attention he knew Sunday would soon show him.

The barking continued.

Sunday pulled back from Josh and feigned surprise.

"That's the guest I want you to meet," Josh said, walking to his bedroom door and opening it.

A smallish German shepherd with a black coat and tan face punctuated by a glistening black nose bounded over to Sunday.

"Oh my gosh, another dog?" Sunday said with exaggerated surprise.

"They think she's two. I decided she could keep Dan company since I'm gone so much."

"I agree." Sunday dropped to her knees to greet the dog. "And you got her—when?"

Josh cleared his throat. "She was at Forever Friends when I met with Frank. He gave me a tour of the facility and … well … we just took to each other."

"I can see why," Sunday said, rubbing the dog's ears. "She's a sweetheart."

"Frank said he would have adopted her if his wife would have let him."

Sunday swung her head around to look at him. "We babysat for their twins, remember? There's no way that family needs another dog right now."

"Right. So, I brought her home with me. For Dan."

"Makes perfect sense." She held the dog's muzzle between her hands. "What's her name?"

"She hasn't got one. I was hoping you'd help me with that."

"She's so pretty." Sunday rocked back on her heels to look at the dog. "Her face looks like a dollop of caramel on top of an espresso. That's it!" She looked up at Josh. "Cara."

"Dan and Cara." Josh looked thoughtful. "They sound good together."

At the sound of his name, Dan pushed his nose under Sunday's arm.

She released Cara and showered attention on Dan. "What do you think of your new friend?"

Dan licked her face.

Sunday sputtered and laughed. "I almost forgot," she said, getting to her feet. "I brought something else with me. Just in case."

She walked to her oversized bucket purse and unzipped it, pulling out a plastic shopping bag bearing the logo of a big box pet store. She removed two squeaky toys—one a squirrel and the other a duck—and turned to the dogs, who were now sitting next to each other, wagging their tails and looking at her expectantly.

"I think Cara gets first choice since she's new." She held out both toys to the shepherd. Cara lunged for the squirrel. Sunday released it and tossed the duck to Dan.

Both dogs pranced around the living room, squeaking their toys.

"How'd you know I'd adopted a dog?" Josh looked at Sunday.

"I never understand how anyone comes away from a shelter without a new pet," Sunday said. "And the entire conversation about your dinner guest not eating pie—that was weird."

She moved closer to Josh so he could hear her above the racket created by the dogs. "She's really sweet—I'm happy for all three of you."

"Thanks."

"I'd love to hear what Frank had to say about the Doggie Day Out program."

"Come outside with me while I grill the steaks," Josh replied, heading for the kitchen. "We can't hear ourselves think in here. Bottom line—he's approved everything I proposed. Frank's already ordered the vests we'll need. They'll arrive Monday. We'll do trial runs for the next two weeks, then publicize it hard before Christmas."

They stepped onto Josh's small back patio, where the grill was already hot. The steaks sizzled when he placed them on the stainless-steel grates.

"How will you get people to volunteer for those first few weeks?"

"All those slots are already filled."

"That was quick!"

"Robert and Lyla will take dogs out for both of those weeks."

"I'm surprised she didn't tell me when I ran into her in the breakroom after lunch."

"She may not know." Josh sounded sheepish. "Robert volunteered them without consulting her."

Sunday considered this. "Lyla will love it. She's been longing to adopt a small dog for months. I'll bet they keep one of the dogs they take out. Who else?"

"Frank's new COO, Neil Parker. He's giving Neil the day off to do it. And his administrative assistant at Haynes Enterprise. Plus, Judy Young and her husband."

"That's a nice turnout."

"There's one more. Maggie recruited them. Alex Scanlon and his partner, Marc."

"The Mayor of Westbury is doing Doggie Day Out?"

"Yep. Great publicity for the program." He flipped the steaks.

"I'd say so. Congratulations. This project is going to be a tremendous success."

"I just hope dogs find new homes because of it."

A rush of warm air hit them as Dan nosed the sliding glass door to the patio open and he and Cara joined them, still squeezing their new toys.

Sunday gestured to Cara with her chin. "I'd say Doggie Day Out can count Cara as its first success."

Josh grinned. He pulled the steaks off the grill, and they all headed inside.

CHAPTER 17

Maggie clicked the button to leave the Zoom room and shut down her computer. The meeting with the outside auditors had gone well. The college's chief financial officer had answered all the questions from his office on the other side of campus. As a forensic accountant by trade, Maggie could tell when someone wasn't sure of an answer and was making things up off the cuff. Their CFO was knowledgeable, accurate, and thorough. She felt confident when she signed off on the CFO's work.

She stood and stretched. It had been a long week. She'd spent most of it reviewing financial statements to prepare for this Zoom meeting.

Maggie checked her watch. It was almost four—too late in the day to start on a new project. She'd leave early and stop at the supermarket on the way home to pick up boneless, skinless chicken thighs and fresh asparagus. John loved them both, and they cooked fast. She'd microwave a packet of frozen brown rice and they'd have a home-cooked meal.

She shrugged into the trench coat she'd worn that morning, before the midday sun had chased away the cold drizzle of the morning, picked up her purse, and headed through the reception area outside her office.

"If there's nothing urgent for me, I'm starting my weekend early," she said as she sailed past Josh's desk.

"Actually ..." He tore his eyes from his computer screen to look at her. "There is."

"Is ... what?"

"Something that might be ... that I think ... is urgent."

Maggie stopped and faced him. "You didn't send me an email while I was on that Zoom about any calls I had to return by the end of the day."

He motioned her to his desk. "I think you need to see this." He turned the screen of his computer so they could both see it.

"What am I looking at?" Maggie asked.

"It's a Facebook post."

Maggie looked away from the screen. "I'm not into social media. The only people I follow are my granddaughters in California and a few friends. I never post anything."

"You need to see this one."

Maggie stooped over to take a better look. "It's that stupid old photo of my late husband, the college president who's got himself in so much trouble now, and those young women. I've seen it. We've dealt with it."

"Read what's written below the picture."

Josh watched her brows pull up and her eyes expand as if they were in a slingshot about to be launched.

"What the hell!" she sputtered.

Josh clicked to the next open tab on his computer. "She's posted the same thing on Instagram."

"This is preposterous! She's saying that her husband isn't guilty of sexual harassment; that the real perpetrator was Paul." Maggie clamped a hand to the top of her head. "She says the women coming forward are blaming her husband because Paul is dead, and they can't get money out of him."

Josh nodded. "Yolanda Yates is painting them as money grubbers."

"Paul did many bad things, but I don't believe he was guilty of sexual harassment."

"He's not here to defend himself," Josh said. "I think you should."

"Yolanda is 'standing by her man.' Surely people will recognize that." Maggie swallowed hard, remembering that time—years ago—when the allegations of Paul's embezzlement had surfaced, and she'd done the same thing. Also mistakenly. "I won't dignify this with a response."

"Honestly, Maggie—I think that's the wrong call here. Social media posts like this can go viral and take on a life of their own. Once that happens, you'll never be able to get the truth out."

Maggie bit her bottom lip and studied the computer screen. "How many people have seen these posts?"

"They both went up 27 minutes ago. As of now, the Facebook post has the most views at 693. Instagram is only 203."

"That's *all*?" Maggie straightened. "If less than a thousand people have seen that, there's nothing to worry about."

"Again, I don't agree. That's a lot of reach for such a short time. She's tagged you in the post. This could get huge in no time."

"Does she mention Highpointe? People are interested in the college, but not me personally."

Josh double-checked the posts on his screen. "Just you. No mention of Highpointe."

"Then I'm not going to worry about it. If things change over the weekend, we'll worry about it on Monday."

He sucked in a breath, and Maggie held up a hand to silence him.

"I'm on the way to pick up something good to cook for dinner. What are your plans for the weekend?" she asked, changing the subject.

"Tomorrow is our first trial for my Doggie Day Out program."

Maggie walked toward the hallway. "I'm impressed you're getting it started so fast."

"This is a trial run," Josh replied. "We hope to gain good exposure for the program. Our first participants are Mayor Scanlon and his partner."

"I love that Alex and Marc are doing this. Will the *Westbury Gazette* write a story about it?"

"They're doing a feature for next Sunday's paper. I hope the dog they take out gets adopted. That'd be perfect."

"It would, indeed. Let's focus our attention on that—on the success of Doggie Day Out—and forget that ridiculous rant from Yolanda Yates."

Josh nodded but didn't comment.

Maggie paused in the doorway. "Frankly, I feel sorry for Yolanda. Her world and family have been torn apart. I know what that feels like. I hope she gets professional help to deal with it all."

"You're kindhearted, Maggie," Josh said as she retreated down the hall. "Too kindhearted."

CHAPTER 18

Alex Scanlon removed the zippered windbreaker and tossed it on the bed.

Marc Benson leaned against the doorframe and looked at his partner. "Oh, for heaven's sake. You're changing your jacket *again*?"

"I'm the mayor, and the press will be there." He slipped into a tweed sport coat with leather patches on the elbows. "I always want to look," he paused, examining his reflection in the full-length mirror, "professional."

"You look professional in that windbreaker," Marc said.

"This coat adds a certain gravitas."

"It adds years, is what it does. It's a nice sport coat—if you were in your seventies. Put it back in our closet for another thirty years."

Alex took one last look at himself and nodded. "This is

the ticket." He looked at his partner. "You've never liked this coat."

"It's fine," Marc said. "I love you, even though you always look like a lawyer everywhere we go. And today, an elderly one."

"I am a lawyer, remember?" Alex walked past him, and they headed for their garage. "Which dog did you pick out for us?"

"We're fifteen minutes from picking him up. Let's allow it to be a surprise."

"Are you secretly hoping we end up adopting him?"

Marc shook his head.

"I thought you said we're finally settled enough to get a dog."

"I did—and I've got one in mind."

"You didn't select the dog you want to adopt for us to spend the day with?"

They got into the car and were soon on their way to Forever Friends.

Marc shook his head. "The whole point of Doggie Day Out is for people in the community to see the dog, fall in love, and go to the shelter to adopt it. I don't want that to happen to the one I want. Besides, you might not want to be seen in front of the camera with the one I like."

Alex groaned. "What have you got your eye on?"

"We had large breeds when I was growing up. I've always favored them."

"Our yard isn't big enough for a dog that requires a lot of room to run."

"And then I met Maggie's dog, Eve," Marc continued. "She's the sweetest dog I've ever come across."

"Eve's a dachshund/terrier mix. Did you find one of those on the Forever Friends website?"

"I did." Marc whipped out his phone and scrolled through the shelter's website.

Alex stopped at a traffic light, and Marc held out the phone to him.

Alex perused the photo of a dog with a pointy dachshund nose, long wiry hair, and espresso-colored eyes.

The light changed, and Alex resumed driving. "How much does he weigh?"

"Fifteen pounds. Something about that serious, soulful expression in his eyes told me he's the one for us." Marc focused on the photo of the little dog on his phone. "He was a stray. They think he's two, based on the condition of his teeth. He's already housebroken, and leash trained."

Alex glanced at his partner. Marc had made up his mind. "What about the dog you've selected for our Doggie Day Out?"

"Sunshine," Marc supplied. "She's a four-year-old golden retriever/poodle mix."

"A golden doodle? I'm surprised no one has adopted her already. Someone will see her out with us today and will want to take her home." He smiled at Marc. "You picked her to make sure Doggie Day Out starts with a roaring success."

"I did," Marc said. "If this works—and we have fun today—I'd like us to do it again. We could bring our little dachshund buddy with us. If we adopt him."

"I have a feeling there's not much doubt about that. We'll be there a few minutes early. Let's go meet this dog before we take out Sunshine. I'm sure they could hold him for us until we return."

"I was hoping you'd say that."

Josh and a staff member of Forever Friends met them at the entrance.

"Sunshine will be ready soon," Josh said. "She's having her breakfast and then we'll put on her vest. The staff member will go over our simple rules."

"Keep her vest and leash on her at all times," the staffer said. "She walks beautifully on a leash, so you won't have any problems. We'd like you to stay within walking distance of the shelter. The park with the Saturday morning farmers market would be a good place to start. After that, there are plenty of coffee shops and boutiques that are dog friendly."

"Even walking her along the street or by the elementary school playground is good," Josh chimed in. "Take her where there are lots of people to see her."

"Is she good with kids and other dogs?" Alex asked.

"She is," the staffer said. "You can encourage people to interact with her."

"If you have any issues, come back to the shelter," Josh said.

"Just make sure no one does anything to her you wouldn't allow to be done to your own dog."

"Speaking of our own dog," Marc said, "we don't have one —yet." He removed his phone from his pocket and pulled up the photo of the little dog that had captured his heart. "Is this guy still available?"

The staffer grinned. "He sure is. That dog is full of personality."

"Is that a good or a bad thing?" Alex asked.

"Good. I promise. We've got a few minutes before Sunshine is ready. Do you want to meet him? This is the perfect time since we're not open to the public for another twenty minutes."

Alex and Marc nodded in unison.

The staffer led them to their destination.

The small pup leapt from a blanket at the back of his kennel and made a beeline for them.

The staffer let the dog out into the aisle. Both men knelt to greet him. The dog sniffed their hands and licked their fingers, his tail swishing like windshield wipers at high speed.

"I can take you to a separate room to get acquainted," the staffer offered.

The dog jumped high, and Alex caught him with the reflexes of a catcher. The dog washed Alex's chin with his tongue.

Alex transferred the squirming bundle to Marc, who stood laughing as his chin received the same treatment.

"I don't think we need more time with this decision," Alex said, locking eyes with Marc.

"We'll take him," Marc said. "Can you save him for us until we return Sunshine this afternoon?"

"I'll put a sign on his kennel right now and we'll have the

adoption paperwork ready and waiting for you. He's a great dog. You won't regret making him part of your family."

Marc held up the dachshund so they were at eye level with each other. "We'll be back for you soon, okay? You're coming home with us. But right now, we're going to help Sunshine find her forever family."

CHAPTER 19

Marc and Alex stood at the entrance to the farmers market, surrounded by families with children of varying ages.

Sunshine sat amid the hubbub, calmly accepting pets, ear rubs, and kisses from all sides.

A couple with three middle-school-aged boys in tow addressed Alex. "You're Mayor Scanlon, aren't you?" the man asked.

Alex extended his hand and introduced himself to the parents.

"I appreciate the initiatives you've implemented around school safety," the mom said. "I feel better about sending my kids to school."

"I'm glad to hear that. Providing a safe environment is crucial to learning." Alex took a breath as he prepared to launch into one of his favorite topics.

"Is this your dog, mister?" one of the boys interrupted to ask Marc.

"Nope. We're just taking him out for the day—so he can spend time away from the shelter."

"That's cool," the boy said, looking at his brothers.

"We want a dog," he continued. His brothers nodded.

"This guy is available to adopt. And there are a lot of others at the shelter who need a good home, too. Alex and I adopted one this morning and we'll pick him up when we return Sunshine."

The boys swung to their parents in one motion. "Please," the youngest said, drawing out the word.

Alex took a flyer featuring Sunshine that the shelter had given him and handed it to the woman. "Whenever you're ready for a new pet, Forever Friends is the place to go."

The woman looked from the pleading eyes of her children back to Alex. "Thank you," she said in a voice that conveyed she didn't really mean it. "You can always sign up for Doggie Day Out to spend time with a dog you're considering," he said. "Make sure you're a good fit."

"That's not a bad idea." The woman brightened at the idea. "For now, we need to head into the market. We're here to buy our organic produce for the week."

The family moved away.

Sunshine continued to be the center of attention as people streamed into the market.

"I can't believe how busy this place is," Alex said.

"The weather report shows a cold front moving in midweek. This may be the last mild day before winter hits in full force."

Alex handed flyers to two additional families and a young couple who were admiring Sunshine. They all moved away, and Sunshine found herself in a momentary lull. Her only admirer was a young boy who watched from a distance, standing ramrod straight next to his mother. His eyes were laser-focused on the friendly dog.

"You can come pet her, if you'd like," Marc said to the boy. "She won't bite."

"My son's fascinated by dogs," the mom said, "but he never wants to touch them."

"Did he have a bad experience with a dog?"

The mother shook her head no. "He's extremely shy. We just put him in preschool and he's finding it …" her voice cracked, "a lot to adjust to. He doesn't engage with anyone other than his dad and me."

The boy continued to stare at Sunshine.

Marc knelt on one knee. "This is Sunshine," he said.

The little boy moved one hand in a barely perceptible wave.

Sunshine turned her head to the boy but didn't lunge for him like she'd done with the other admiring children that morning.

"Would you like to tell her your name?" Marc asked.

"Timothy." The boy squeaked out his name.

Sunshine thumped her tail against the ground in what seemed like acknowledgement.

The boy chuckled.

His mother took a step back.

"She loves to have her ears rubbed." Marc demonstrated, and Sunshine pressed her head into Marc's hand.

The boy grinned.

"Would you like to try it?"

The boy slowly tilted his face to his mother's.

"It's okay," she said. "That nice doggy won't hurt you. I bet he'll feel like your stuffed animals." She glanced at Marc and Alex. "His bed is covered with them."

"I had stuffed animals when I was your age," Marc said. "Sunshine is like one of them, only better because she's real." He continued to stroke the dog's ears.

Sunshine kept her gaze steady on the boy.

The boy took a tentative step forward, followed by another. He reached Sunshine's side, then stopped, his arms clamped to his sides.

"Can I take your hand in mine, and we'll pet Sunshine together?" Marc asked.

The boy nodded.

Marc covered the boy's tiny hand with his own and slowly brought them to the top of Sunshine's head. Together, they rubbed her ears.

Marc eased his hand away, and the boy continued to pet Sunshine, adding his other hand to the task. Before long, he was moving them along the dog's back.

Sunshine turned her muzzle to the boy and gave him a gentle kiss.

The boy stopped moving, and his features froze.

His mother drew in a sharp breath but waited for her son's reaction.

The boy's frown dissolved like footprints on a sandy beach. He threw his arms around Sunshine and hugged her, burying his face in the fur of her neck.

"I've ... he's ... never," the boy's mother sputtered, bringing her hand to her heart.

The three adults watched the touching scene in front of them as Sunshine covered the boy's face and arms with kisses. The only sound was the infectious laughter of a happy child.

"He certainly loves your dog," the mother said when she'd regained her composure. "I've never seen anyone get through to my son like Sunshine."

"They definitely have a special connection," Alex said. "But she's not our dog." He pointed to the vest that Sunshine wore and explained the program. He concluded by handing her one of the flyers.

"You mean we could adopt her? She could be ours?"

Marc and Alex nodded.

"Oh, my gosh! Have you been here all morning?"

Both men nodded again.

"I'll bet you've been mobbed. Has anyone else said they wanted to adopt her?"

"I think several families are interested," Marc said.

The woman extended her hand to her son. "We have to go, honey."

He reluctantly released Sunshine and turned toward the entrance to the market.

"We're skipping the market today." She took his hand and pulled him to her. "I think we should go to the shelter to adopt Sunshine. Don't you?"

A smile ripped across the boy's face with seismic force.

"I just pray that no one's beat us to it," she said to Marc and Alex as they hurried away.

"We do, too," Marc called after her.

Alex whipped out his cell phone. "I think we can help with that." He placed a call to Forever Friends. The growing smile on his face signaled no one had come in, yet, to adopt Sunshine, and the shelter would hold her until the mother and little boy who Alex described came in, as long as it was before the end of the day.

CHAPTER 20

Marc approached the group of children surrounding the tall, thin man in the sport coat. The recyclable canvas bag looped over his elbow swung freely. The vegetable stand was sold out of almost everything on his list by the time he and Alex had decided they'd never make it there together with Sunshine at their side. Marc had gone alone.

"Success?" Alex looked over the heads of the children playing with the dog.

"If you call three apples and an acorn squash success."

Alex rolled his eyes. "I've got good news."

Marc arched his brows.

"The shelter called, and Sunshine's been adopted."

"The mother and that shy little boy?"

Alex nodded.

"That's great news!"

"They're coming back at four-thirty to pick him up."

Marc checked his watch. "It's three-thirty now. What time will the newspaper reporter show up for photos?"

"She came while you were gone. I got the call from Forever Friends when she was here. Boy, was she excited! She said this story will make a perfect Sunday feature. She's going to meet us at the shelter at four-thirty to capture us returning Sunshine and the new family adopting her."

"I love the sound of that! Let's walk up the block, past the coffee shop and the boutiques, before we head to the shelter to give extra exposure to the program."

"Good idea. We've got plenty of time."

The threesome peeled off as the crowd dissipated from the now-closed farmers market.

Sunshine continued to receive admiring looks from everyone they passed, but no one stopped them. They were approaching the coffee shop when two familiar figures stepped out onto the sidewalk.

Maggie and Susan had met for a cup of coffee to complete plans for the Thanksgiving potluck. The close-knit mother and daughter usually saw eye-to-eye on almost everything. Today, however, they were clearly not in agreement. Susan was wagging her finger in front of Maggie's face and Maggie was shaking her head. Both women were talking at once.

Marc and Alex halted.

"What's this?" Marc asked. He turned wide eyes to Alex.

"Looks like a mother-daughter squabble," Alex replied.

Susan raised her voice, and they heard the word "ridiculous."

"Uh-oh," Alex said. "I don't want any part of this."

"Me neither. Let's cross the street and walk back on the other side."

They were approaching the crosswalk when Susan spotted them. "Marc. ALEX!" she called.

The men turned toward her.

She motioned them over with a vigorous roll of her hand. "You've got to hear this," she said as they joined her and Maggie.

"My mother is …" she bit her lip, searching for the right word.

"I'm simply viewing a set of circumstances differently than my daughter."

"Your lawyer daughter, Mom. And these circumstances could have legal implications—or at least do reputational damage."

"I'm sure—" Alex began.

"Look at this post on social media," Susan interjected, holding out her phone to Alex.

He read the post that Josh had pointed out to Maggie the afternoon before, then whistled softly. He passed the phone to Marc, who scrolled through the post and the comments.

"Well. What do you think?" Susan asked.

"It's not good. Not at all. How have you responded?" Alex addressed Maggie.

"See?!" Susan spun on her mother, a note of triumph in her voice.

Maggie sighed in exasperation. "I haven't responded at all. It's just some stupid thing on social media. Nobody takes that stuff seriously."

"The Facebook post has a reach of almost 150,000," Marc pointed out quietly. "And there are over 1,000 comments. I obviously haven't had time to read more than a handful of them, but they're very critical, nasty even."

"We have to get the PR people involved, Mom. You should have called them yesterday afternoon."

"It was after hours," Maggie said. "I didn't want to bother them."

"Firms that handle this sort of issue know that things like this don't happen during business hours. You should have called me, too. I had to find it scrolling through Facebook." She looked at Alex. "Tell her."

Alex cleared his throat. "I agree with Susan. You need a strategy to handle this. Paul may be gone, but you were married to him at the time. Now that you're a public figure, this is going to blow back on you."

Maggie's face turned red, and her eyes flashed. "You're making a mountain out of a molehill." She stared at Susan and then Alex.

Marc reached out and touched her shoulder lightly. "I can imagine how annoying this situation is," he said calmly. "It's hurtful, and it's unfair. But—for what it's worth—I think Susan and Alex are correct. It may already be too late to nip this in the bud, but you need to address it."

Maggie wilted like a cut flower out of water. "All right. You win. I'll call the PR team on Monday."

"Email them tomorrow," Susan said. "That way, they'll have it first thing Monday morning. I'll come over to help you."

"You'll do no such thing." Maggie bristled at the suggestion. "I can handle a simple email."

"Okay." Susan held her hands up. "Don't get your back up. I was just offering."

Maggie glared at her. "Or trying to control me. I told you. I'll send an email tomorrow."

"Fine." The two women stared at each other.

"Have you met our friend Sunshine?" Marc asked, attempting to break the tension. "We're on our way back to Forever Friends after the first ever Doggie Day Out."

Maggie looked at the sweet pup sitting patiently at Marc's side.

"Josh told me about the program. He's so excited about it. Tell us how it went today."

Alex recounted their day, saving the happy news that Sunshine was going to her forever family as soon as they returned to the shelter. "Speaking of which, we need to get going."

The two men and the dog continued on their way, leaving a calmer scene behind them.

CHAPTER 21

John deposited his shop vac at the bottom of the stairs and brushed the dust from the front of his shirt. Maggie would be pleased that he'd moved the furniture in the attic into accessible rows. He'd hauled two standing shop lights up the steep steps so Gordon could see the items he was coming from New York City to examine. Although Maggie hadn't asked him to vacuum the dust, he'd done his best to make the attic a more palatable place for the appraiser to spend the upcoming week.

He expected to find her in the library, reading in the oversized chair by the French doors leading to the garden. That's what she'd told their friends Joan and Sam Torres she'd be doing after church that morning. Both women had agreed that the book club pick for this month was difficult to get into and they needed to spend the afternoon reading.

Maggie was nowhere to be seen. Roman and Eve—who never let Maggie out of their sight—weren't in their beds by the hearth. The book sat on the table next to the chair. The lamp on the table was off.

A rhythmic thumping noise drew John to the kitchen. Roman raised his head in greeting when John entered the room, but Eve continued napping in her basket in the breakfast nook.

Maggie stood at the kitchen island. She wore one of the quilted aprons she'd purchased in Linden Falls. Flour dusted the fall leaves and pumpkins printed on the fabric. She picked up a large piece of dough, scattered flour on the surface in front of her, slapped the dough down, and kneaded it, the heels of her hands pushing it with considerable force.

"Here you are."

Maggie glanced up at him quickly before picking up the dough again and repeating the process. "Yes. Here I am."

John sucked in a breath. He knew his wife all too well—she escaped to the kitchen when she was extremely happy or agitated and upset. Based on her response to him and the vengeance with which she was attacking the dough, he knew she was upset.

"Still stewing about that stupid social media post?"

Maggie gave him an icy stare. "And my confrontation with Susan."

"The one she roped Alex and Marc into?"

Maggie swiped an errant strand of hair off her face, leaving a streak of flour on her forehead. "Exactly. I don't need my daughter to share my business with everyone in town."

John stepped cautiously toward her. "Marc and Alex are hardly 'everyone in town.'" He stood next to her. "Susan is concerned about you, honey. I understand you hate the whole situation, but don't take it out on Susan."

Maggie gave the dough one last push, then shaped it into an oblong and placed it in a greased pan. She covered it with an old tea towel and set it aside to rise. Maggie faced him, her fisted hand resting on her hip.

"I get that she's looking out for me, but shouldn't she give me a little more credit for knowing how to handle this?"

"She *is* an attorney…"

"I know that," Maggie snapped. "And I'm a forensic accountant, a previous mayor of this town, and a college president. Maybe—just maybe—everyone should back off and let me handle this my way." She glared at him.

John reached out a hand and gently brushed the flour off her forehead with his thumb. "You are all those things—and so much more."

Maggie's rigid posture softened. "You have confidence in me?"

"Always," John said. "Consider their advice, then make up your own mind."

"Thank you," Maggie said. She glanced at her apron. "I'd hug you, but I'd get flour all over you."

John pulled her into him. "I couldn't care less about a little flour." He bent to kiss her.

The buzzer on the oven sounded. Maggie pushed back and slipped out of his embrace. "That'll be my apple crisp," she said, reaching for her oven mitts.

"I smelled that the minute I walked into the kitchen. I thought you bought a dessert at Laura's yesterday. Dinner tonight would be easy. I was going to grill steaks."

"That was the plan. It all changed when we got home from church. I started in on our book club book and couldn't concentrate on it. I kept thinking about things and, before I knew it, I was in here." She waved her arm around the kitchen. "I've got rosemary sourdough bread rising for toast and sandwiches this week. Our first course will be a mixed greens salad with candied pears and spiced pecans. Instead of steaks, I've prepped a stuffed crown roast of pork, and we'll have it with sautéed Brussels sprouts."

John patted his stomach. "Wow."

"We'll finish with the choice of Laura's pumpkin pie or my apple crisp."

"Or a serving of each?" John tilted his head to one side.

Maggie laughed. "Yes. Of course."

"Your cooking is always wonderful—one of the many reasons I'm such a lucky man." He grinned at her. "I shouldn't feel this way, but I'm grateful that Yolanda Yates stirred up so much trouble."

Maggie narrowed her eyes at him.

"If she hadn't, you'd be reading a book you don't like, and we wouldn't be eating such a remarkable dinner tonight."

Maggie cuffed him on the shoulder.

He took a step back. "I'm just saying—you're the only person I know whose anger turns into something so productive."

CHAPTER 22

The doorbell chimes of Rosemont propelled Roman and Eve out of their baskets. Their chorus of half-warning, half-welcoming barks preceded them as they tore toward the front door.

Maggie dried her hands on a towel and untied her apron, slinging it on the kitchen counter.

She and John met in the foyer. The dogs sat in the place near the door where they had been trained to wait, and John opened the massive mahogany front door.

A tall, slim man with a trim haircut stood on the welcome mat. Even though he'd arrived after a long drive, his trousers still held a neat crease and his blue, button-down shirt remained nicely starched.

"Gordon!" Maggie opened her arms wide and swept him into an embrace.

After a moment of awkward stiffness, the man returned her warm hug.

"We're so glad you're here," Maggie said. "We've been looking forward to your visit."

"Thank you, madam," he replied, stepping out of her arms.

"Maggie! I swear, Gordon—if you call me 'madam' one more time…"

He held up his hands. "I know. I'm sorry. I'm an old dog learning a new trick." He smiled at her. "Maggie," he said.

She patted him on the back.

Gordon turned to John and extended his hand.

The two men shook.

"Good trip?" John asked, ushering Gordon into the house and closing the door.

"Delightful. Fall foliage was past its peak where I started out, but, as I headed west, all that changed. Leaves were at their prime and the weather was clear and sunny the whole way. I couldn't have had a prettier drive."

"That's wonderful," Maggie said. "You even got here a few hours earlier than expected."

"I hope that's not a problem, mad, um, Maggie."

"Not in the least. We told you we'd be home all day."

Gordon bent and greeted the dogs, who swept the floor with their tails but remained in their sitting position.

"Would you like to settle into your room?" Maggie asked. "We've got another couple of hours before dinner."

"I want to change, and then I'd like to get into the attic," Gordon said. "I've been looking forward to this for weeks."

"Sure," John said. "Where are your bags?"

"In the car."

"I'll help you carry them up to your room. I've moved stuff around in the attic to make it easier for you to evaluate its contents. Once you're ready to start, come get me in the library and I'll go to the attic with you."

"Excellent," Gordon said, rubbing his hands together.

"I'll bring you both water bottles, and then I'll be in the kitchen if either of you needs anything." Maggie signaled to the dogs, and they retreated as John and Gordon headed to Gordon's car.

∽

Maggie took the crown roast of pork out of the oven and set it on the kitchen counter to rest. Everything else was ready. By the time they'd eaten their salads, the roast would be ready to carve.

She looked over at Eve and Roman. They were now sitting upright and alert in their baskets. Both noses twitched at warp speed, taking in the delicious aroma of roasted meat.

"I think the two of you had better go outside while I head upstairs to tell John and Gordon that dinner is ready."

Roman rolled his soulful eyes to hers.

"I know you're a good boy," she said, "but there's no sense tempting fate. Eve isn't tall enough to get onto the counters, but you are." She patted her leg as she walked by them to the kitchen door.

They reluctantly abandoned their beds and went into the back garden.

Maggie retraced her steps and met up with John and Gordon on the stairs. "I was just coming to get you."

"We could smell that dinner was ready," John said.

"I hope you're hungry, Gordon," Maggie said. "I got carried away in the kitchen today."

"I am, indeed." He lifted his head and inhaled. "Pork?"

"Yes. Is that all right? I should have asked you first."

"It's a favorite, in fact. One I rarely indulge."

"Good." Maggie led them to the dining room. "We'll start with our salads and then I'll serve family style from the kitchen."

The meal was soon underway, with congenial conversation accompanying the delicious food.

At Maggie's urging, Gordon recounted the auction in London of the Van Cleef & Arpels brooch that had provided seed money for Forever Guides, the guide dog training school that Frank Haynes planned to open next to Forever Friends.

"That must have been a fascinating experience," John said.

"It was a highlight of my professional life," Gordon said.

"Matching the auction proceeds from your personal funds, Gordon" —Maggie caught his gaze and held it— "was extraordinarily kind."

Gordon shook his head and opened his mouth to speak.

"Don't deny it," John interjected. "We know you're the anonymous matching donor. We won't say anything about it if you want to remain that way, but, within these four walls, we both want to acknowledge you for your generosity."

Gordon flushed and looked at the tablecloth.

"How's the cleaning and restoration of the Thomas Cole painting coming along?" Maggie asked. Their guest clearly wasn't comfortable being praised.

Gordon jerked his head up. "Brilliantly," he replied. "The cleaning is done, and there are only a handful of spots that need to be restored. It's absolutely breathtaking."

Maggie clasped her hands together. "I'm delighted to hear that. Do you think it'll do well at auction?"

Gordon leaned back in his chair and looked from Maggie to John. "I'm certain of it." He hesitated before continuing. "I'd like you to see it again before you decide to sell it. In fact, I recommend you rehang it above the main fireplace and live with it for six months."

"But we've got the painting we bought on our honeymoon in Cornwall over that fireplace," Maggie protested.

"I think that would work much better in the library. The proportions are better there."

"Isn't the Cole too valuable for us to keep?" John asked.

"I've given that a lot of thought," Gordon said. "It's a valuable piece, to be sure. But this is a grand old house and was home to the painting for decades. Maybe it should come back here."

Maggie and John stared at him in silence.

"Insurance on the painting is affordable," he continued. "My quick assessment of the furniture in your attic is that you have some very fine pieces. But none of it is museum quality. You can insure all of it."

"Not like the Martin-Guillaume Biennais tea set you found up there before?"

"No. That was truly extraordinary. You did the right thing to sell that."

"Particularly since the proceeds allowed us to buy out Frank Haynes' interest in Rosemont," Maggie said. "What should we do with all that furniture?"

Gordon smiled at her. "Do you watch *Antiques Roadshow*?"

Maggie laughed. "Doesn't everybody?"

"I'm going to tell you what those appraisers say to people who bring in objects they've had in their homes for decades without knowing how valuable they are: enjoy them. Bring them downstairs and use them."

"I've already got a lot of furniture down here."

"Do you like all of it?"

Maggie and John looked at each other.

"Not *all* of it."

"I can help you assess what to keep and what to replace. Together, John and I can bring the pieces down from the attic. I'll assist you in placing them."

Maggie sat back in her chair. "I *do* love to change things up once in a while."

"You see? It'll be fun," Gordon said. "Why don't we take a quick peek in the attic after dinner?"

"The two of you can go up there now." John stood and began collecting their plates. "I'll clear the table and clean the kitchen. By the time you're done, we'll be ready for dessert."

Maggie pushed back her chair. "I'd like to do that. Thank you, John." She headed to the staircase with Gordon on her heels.

Twenty minutes later, they'd looked at all the furniture and traded ideas on possible placements on the two floors below. Gordon was turning off the shop lights when a lid from an old-fashioned dish barrel flew off with a noisy pop. He started.

Maggie cast a quick glance around the attic.

They both made their way to the barrel.

Gordon reached in and pulled out an exquisite china plate with a wide scrolled pattern in gold leaf. He handed it to Maggie and removed another identical plate. "Royal Crown Derby," he said.

"It's gorgeous," Maggie replied in a hushed voice. She turned the plate over and checked the mark on the back. Gordon was correct.

"It looks like your attic has some additional secrets for us, after all," Gordon said.

Maggie searched the shadows of the attic once more. "I think you're right."

She took the second plate from him, and they returned to the dining room where John had their dessert plates dished up and waiting for them.

CHAPTER 23

Alistair:

I thought I was alone for the night. To be truthful, I had *hoped* I would be alone. John and the man called Gordon, who had been in the attic several times since Maggie moved in, had rooted around up here for most of the afternoon. After decades of solitary Sundays in the Rosemont attic, I liked the peace and quiet.

I'd heard Maggie talking to them on the stairs. They'd acknowledged that the delicious aromas of the dinner she was making had reached them. They were headed downstairs, hoping it was time to eat.

When we'd had company for dinner at Rosemont back in my time, the meal would comprise at least six courses: soup, salad, fish, meat, cheese, and dessert. The entire affair lasted for hours and no one would have had the energy or inclination for a trip to the attic afterward.

Imagine my surprise when footsteps on the attic steps roused me an hour or two later.

Gordon picked up a yellow pad of paper, with several pages turned back on themselves, and led Maggie from one piece of furniture to the next.

I hovered close by to hear what he was saying. I knew these pieces of furniture like the back of my hand. The master and mistress had undertaken European buying trips to bring most of them home to furnish Rosemont.

Gordon occasionally glanced at his notes but spoke mostly from an expertise that impressed me. The man was correct in every detail. He knew his stuff.

I was thankful Maggie agreed with his suggestion to use the furniture downstairs. That's where it all belonged. He'd offered to help her find places for it. I, of course, knew where it should go. I'd have to find a way to insert myself into those decisions.

They were turning to leave when I had some fun with them. My sojourns downstairs had assured me that Maggie loved fine china. One of the first things she'd done when she'd taken up residence was to wash all the china and clean the butler's pantry. That she'd prioritized restoring the room that had been my pride and joy—well—it still brought me to tears.

She'd never noticed the dish barrel in a dark recess of the attic. It was time I changed that. Unless I'd lost my ability to assess people, I expected she was going to adore our collection of Royal Crown Derby.

They were turning out the lights when I finally dislodged

the cantankerous lid from the barrel and sent it clattering noisily to the floor.

They'd responded to this disturbance by peeking into the barrel.

Maggie's reaction—her widening eyes and shallow breathing—told me I'd been right. She'd taken a couple of plates downstairs with her, but I knew by the look in her eyes that she'd be back in the attic—and soon—to uncover the entire contents of the barrel.

CHAPTER 24

Maggie turned the collar of her trench coat up as she walked. The wind at her back held the distinct promise of winter. She made a mental note to zip in the fleece lining of her coat when she got home.

She valued her habit of taking a midday stroll across campus. Saying hello to students and faculty as she passed by them enhanced her connection to the college community. Her efforts were appreciated. Student surveys give her high marks for being approachable and in touch with their daily lives.

On days like today, when the weather discouraged leisurely outings, Maggie did a lot of thinking. She'd often ruminate on a nagging issue while she walked, and usually came up with a solution.

Today, she focused on the social media posts put up by Yolanda Yates. As irritating and unfair as they were, she understood the woman's heartbreak over Malcolm's betrayal. If even half of the accusations against him were true, he was an immoral monster.

Yolanda must feel like she's on a tilt-a-wheel ride at the fair, Maggie thought. *She's feeling like she's drowning and is thrashing about, looking for a lifeline.*

Maggie shook her head. Susan was correct—she felt sorry for Yolanda. Susan was also right that she had to stop Yolanda's unfounded allegations against Maggie's late husband, Paul.

Maggie cast her mind back to the conference earlier this year where she'd served as a panelist. Yolanda had slipped into the back of the room for the sole purpose of asking questions designed to discredit Maggie.

At the time, Maggie had been livid. She'd wanted to lash out. The moderator of the panel had discounted and dismissed Yolanda's snarky statements. Her colleague and former president of Highpointe, Ian Lawry, had advised her to ignore Yolanda and her accusations. He had said it would all blow over. She'd heeded his advice, and it had. If she'd addressed Yolanda's comments, she'd have drawn attention to issues no one was concerned with.

Wasn't Maggie in the same situation now? Should she really unleash her PR team and lawyer on a devastated and broken woman?

Maggie pursed her lips. There was a reason she was hesitant to respond publicly. Her gut told her not to. And she was going to listen to her gut.

Maggie quickened her pace back to her office. She knew what she was going to do.

∼

MAGGIE PRESSED the Do Not Disturb button on her desk phone. She wanted to craft her email without interruption.

Maggie searched through old strings of emails she'd received in connection with conferences she'd attended as the wife of a college president. People weren't as conscientious about hiding recipient's emails from each other back then. She decided on the walk back to her office that, if she found an email address for Yolanda Yates, she'd forego the PR firm and attorney and contact the woman directly. If she didn't, she'd contact her advisors, as Susan and Alex had recommended.

She found an address for Yolanda and took that as a sign she was doing the right thing.

Maggie leaned over her personal laptop and reread, for the sixth time, what she'd written. Her message was clear and her tone empathetic, but firm.

Yolanda,

I'm deeply sorry for the pain you and your family must be feeling right now. I know how awful it is to have allegations like this aired in public.

As you navigate your way through these unchartered waters, I ask that you stop lashing out at innocent parties. Paul had nothing to do with any of the allegations being made against Malcolm.

If you choose to defend your husband, please do so without implicating Paul. He is, after all, no longer able to defend himself.

I hope you are surrounded by supportive people who are giving you the help you need. I pray that you and yours come out of this dark time to a place of peace.

Respectfully,

Maggie

She inhaled slowly, pressed send, and then released the Do Not Disturb button on her phone. She picked up the receiver and began listening to her voice messages. Only one of them required a return call. A member of the board of trustees asked that Maggie give him a quick call.

The trustee was an officious man who rarely prepared for their board meetings and paid poor attention to their discussions, frequently asking for points to be repeated. Maggie sucked in a deep breath. Whatever it was he wanted to discuss, she was sure there was something in it for him.

She placed the call. He wanted to discuss the rejection of his grandson's application for mid-year admission. "As you said yourself," she kept her voice calm, "your grandson's standardized test scores were far below our requirements."

She listened to his response. "I agree that standardized tests are not a perfect barometer of a student's success in college. That's why we factor in their high school grades. A 2.25 GPA is not high enough to overcome substandard test scores."

She let him talk. "Yes—high performance in community college can overcome all this. We recognize that maturity plays a significant part in a student's success. Some high schoolers grow up when they hit college and do exceedingly well. Your grandson hasn't received his grades from his first semester of community college. Even assuming they're straight As, we wouldn't admit him."

The man cut her off.

"I know how anxious you are for him to follow in your family's footsteps at Highpointe," she said. "And I'm aware that you're a trustee." Her voice grew icy. "All the more reason to stick by our rules. Pulling strings for him won't do him any favors in the long run. And I won't allow the college to compromise its standards. That would be a dereliction of my duty."

Her jawline tightened as she listened to his response. "We'll have to agree to disagree, then," she said in even tones before hanging up the phone.

Maggie was about to refill her coffee cup from the coffeemaker in her reception area when her eyes landed on her laptop. The screen showed she had an email reply from Yolanda Yates in her inbox.

She sat back down in her chair and opened it.

I wondered if I'd receive an email from the sanctimonious Maggie Martin. I guess you would know how I feel—except my husband did nothing wrong! We can't say the same about Paul. I've even heard rumors he had a second family. My, my—that must have been a "dark time" for you.

Save your prayers for yourself.

Y

Maggie slapped her open palm on the desk. What was *wrong* with people? First the trustee and now this nastygram from Yolanda. No wonder the other college president's wives—including herself—found the woman patronizing and arrogant. She'd now add insufferable to that list.

She reached for her coffee cup, then thrust it aside. She wouldn't put up with Yolanda's mean-spirited nonsense. Her fingers flew across her keypad.

I'm sorry—but not surprised—by your petty response. Your reputation among the wives as being self-serving and uncooperative is well deserved.

My point remains: leave Paul out of it.

Malcolm is entitled to defend himself. Because of the sheer volume of complaints and the number of accusers, I highly doubt he is innocent. Given that, I will continue to pray for you and your kids.

M

Maggie paused, her hand hovering above the keyboard. It wasn't like her to send out a curt reply. Maybe, she thought, now was the time to start. If she wasn't such a nice, accommodating person, the trustee might not have leaned on her to violate admission policies. She hit the send button.

It was high time for everyone to see a new side of Maggie Martin.

CHAPTER 25

Gordon walked past the glass door with the words Archer's Bridal lettered in a flourishy gold script. He continued to the plate-glass window to admire the display. A mannequin wearing a stunning Alencon lace ballgown-style dress occupied the center front of the window.

A chair upholstered in white damask stood to the left of the mannequin. The seat held a pair of jeweled pumps and a matching evening bag. The item on the right, however, captured Gordon's attention.

A vintage treadle sewing machine sat open and ready for use on top of an ornate Victorian wooden cabinet.

A chilly gust tore one end of his scarf off his neck, and he grasped it, securing the ends inside the lapels of his coat before it blew away from him. He tied his coat tighter around him and leaned toward the window for a better look at the machine.

The ironwork above the treadle prominently displayed the word Singer and the name was written in gold-leaf letters on the machine itself. Decorative decals with elaborate gold, red, blue, and green details adorned the glossy, black surface of the cast iron machine.

The cabinet contained a row of five narrow drawers on either side of the central area that supported the machine when it was in position for use or protected it when stored inside the cabinet. The wood grain gleamed with golden highlights. Carvings around every drawer pull spoke of fine cabinetmaker details.

The machine and cabinet were immaculate. His pulse quickened. He was a connoisseur of beautiful, old objects—particularly when they'd been well cared for.

Gordon was leaning to his right to examine the side of the cabinet when Anita opened the door to the shop that had been in her family for decades.

"You'll catch your death out here." She gestured for him to come inside. "It's in the twenties now and the forecast says a cold front is on the way. This is as warm as it's going to get today, and we'll be in the single digits overnight."

"Thank you," Gordon said as he stepped inside. "I didn't think it would be this cold before Thanksgiving." He combed his hair into place with his fingers. "I should have packed a hat."

Anita shut the door behind them and held out her hands

for his coat. "There's a very nice men's store across the square," she said. "It'll have more formal—and expensive—hats. You can find a practical knit cap at the sporting goods store in the mall on the outskirts of town."

"I appreciate the information," he said, depositing his coat across her arm.

"I'll hang this in our employee coat closet. Through here," she said, leading him into the sewing workroom.

Rows of unadorned windows along two walls and a network of long, fluorescent fixtures illuminated the spacious room. Classical music played softly in the background. Four large, elevated worktables occupied the room. Two women, clad in white, sat on stools or stood at the side of each table. They each wore cloth tape measures around their necks and pin cushion wrist corsages. Scissors and oversized spools of thread were scattered across the tables. A wedding gown lay in the center of each one.

The women, focused on their painstaking work, didn't look up as Anita and Gordon passed by.

"What a calm atmosphere," he remarked.

Anita chuckled. "Most of the time, it is."

He raised an eyebrow. "Oh?"

"Things can get a bit …" she hesitated, choosing her words, "tense, when a bride comes in for a fitting and everything's not perfect."

"It looks like you've got a team of pros out there." He glanced toward the workroom. "I'll bet that doesn't happen often."

"If a bride has gained or lost weight since her last fitting, that's when we run into problems."

"Gosh—what do you do?"

"You'd be amazed at the skill of those women. We always come up with something." She smiled at him. "You didn't come here to talk about bridal alterations. Would you like to see the rest of my stash of old sewing machines?"

"Very much. Are they all in the same condition as the one in the window?"

Anita shook her head. "I've restored many, but not all of them. It's an ongoing labor of love."

"The one in the window appears to be superb," he said. "Did you work on that one?"

Anita flushed at the compliment on her work. "I did. I learned to sew on that old machine. It remains my favorite."

"Tell me about it," Gordon said.

"It's a Singer model 15K. My grandmother bought it for its durability. We used it in the shop until she passed away in 1980. I've still got the original bill of sale from 1939. It was manufactured in the 1930s, in Scotland."

"Wow. That's terrific provenance. Is the cabinet original?"

Anita nodded.

"And it still works?"

"Absolutely. Sewing machines that are a hundred years old—even a hundred fifty—are still in use today. I'm part of a Facebook group for fans of vintage sewing machines. They're durable, completely repairable, strong, and eco-friendly."

"And beautiful," Gordon supplied.

"Yes. Very much so."

"How did you learn to restore them?"

"My grandmother taught me how to repair almost every machine I've got. We used most of them in the shop. I've acquired a few more over the years." Anita sighed. "The collecting bug has bitten me. Whenever I run across an old sewing machine at an estate or garage sale, I snap it up. I've snagged some beauties, I can tell you."

"I can't wait to see."

She hung his coat in the closet and opened a door next to it. "Everything's in the basement."

She ushered him down a steep flight of stairs to a small, tidy room. The same fluorescent fixtures that illuminated the sewing workroom provided ample light in the basement. A workbench containing precise rows of tools stood against one wall. Wire racks filled with neatly arranged sewing machines lined two other walls. Six sewing cabinets were pushed up against the fourth wall.

Anita busied herself at the large, rectangular worktable in the center of the space while Gordon slowly walked along the shelves of sewing machines. He whistled softly. "These are remarkable. I thought you said you hadn't restored all of them." He turned to her.

Anita shrugged. "Some of them need more work."

"You, madam, are a perfectionist," he said in a voice that conveyed his approval.

"Thank you."

He joined her at the table and removed the satchel slung over his shoulder. "May I?" He nodded at the table. "I don't want to disturb you, but I'd like a small space for my computer and cameras."

"Sure." She stacked the set of ten identical small plastic bins in front of her. "I was just sorting things into these bins for the Girl Scouts."

"You're a Girl Scout leader, too?"

"No. Once a year, I teach a class for girls working on their sewing badge."

"That's nice of you."

"I enjoy it. And I feel it's very useful." She cocked her head to one side. "Do you know how to sew on a button, Gordon?"

"I do. And I can mend a ripped seam. My mother made sure of it. She always said there are certain skills in life everyone must have."

"I couldn't agree with her more. Since they stopped teaching home economics in the schools, people don't know how to do those things anymore. The alterations business is flourishing for dry cleaners because nobody can do it themselves. I guess it's a good thing since people aren't buying dry-cleanable clothes these days. They need the revenue stream. Sometimes I wonder if I should offer a class on basic mending."

Gordon nodded. "Have you ever thought about teaching people how to restore sewing machines?"

"I get calls about that all the time. The Singer has been in the window for years. That started it." Anita chuckled. "Maybe I should. You've given me something to think about."

She headed for the stairs. "I've got a fitting in ten

minutes. I'd better get up there and leave you to do your thing." She paused with her foot on the bottom rung. "Where are my manners? Would you like a cup of coffee?"

"That would be most appreciated." He followed her up the stairs. "Just show me where to find it and I'll help myself."

CHAPTER 26

Gordon packed up his satchel by mid-afternoon. He retrieved his coat from the closet and found Anita in the workroom. "I'm going to head to Pete's. Maggie said it functions as a coffee shop in the afternoons," he said.

Anita put her hand to the side of her head. "You must be starved. I didn't think of that. I rarely eat lunch."

"Nor do I. I've completed photographing and cataloging your collection. I'd like to do some online research on values and make a few phone calls to other knowledgeable appraisers."

"Any preliminary thoughts?" Anita rocked from foot to foot, telegraphing the eagerness she didn't convey in her calm voice.

Gordon pursed his lips and looked into her hopeful face.

"Not quite yet," he said in an even tone. "I should have a rough estimate of value by the end of the afternoon."

Anita clasped her hands together.

"Would you like me to stop by later?"

"I've got a better idea," Anita said. "I'll drop by Pete's as soon as I close up. I should be there by 6:15. Maybe you can give me your findings over dinner?"

"That's an excellent idea, madam," he replied. Gordon truthfully thought it was a terrible idea. He'd already concluded that, although her collection was in remarkable condition and contained a few rare pieces, most of it was fairly pedestrian. The Singer K15 in the window might bring $1,000 at auction due to the pristine condition of the cabinet. Her Singer 66k Lotus in the basement was her crown jewel. If it was worth more than $3,000, he would be shocked.

Dashing people's hopes—telling them that their cherished family heirloom held only practical or sentiment value, but little to no monetary worth—was the worst part of his job.

He looked again into her eager face. He liked Anita Archer. She was smart, industrious, and valued beautiful objects. He hated that her collection wouldn't provide a comfortable retirement for her.

"See you soon," he said as he strode out the door, casting one glance back at her. Maybe he could think of another way her collection could delight her.

Anita finished her Chicken Marsala and put her fork on her plate. "I never knew that the Singer Sewing Machine Company was the largest furniture manufacturer in the world over a hundred years ago."

"It's fascinating, from a business perspective." Gordon took a swig of water. "Sewing machines were heavy affairs made of cast iron and steel—a far cry from the portable plastic models you see today. They had to be supported by a sturdy piece of furniture. By 1900, Singer had two factories. Records only exist for one of them. It employed 3,000 woodworkers who produced over two million cabinets a year. The other factory probably did the same. Singer revolutionized woodworking and mass production." He coughed and reached for his glass.

Anita leaned across the table and touched his hand. "You've clearly learned a lot about the history of sewing machines, and I'd like to hear more, but I'm dying for you to tell me what you think of my collection. The fact that you haven't said a word about it through the entire meal"—she gestured to their cleaned entrée plates— "makes me … nervous."

Gordon's face grew red from his collar to his temples, and he shifted his gaze to where their hands touched. "I'm sorry, madam … Anita." He lifted his eyes to meet hers. "Of course you want to know. I frequently do this—deliver news that people don't want to hear. I hate disappointing people, but I especially don't want to upset you. That's why I was stalling."

Anita smiled at him. "You're still stalling. I'm prepared for whatever it is. I assure you I won't burst into tears or make a scene."

He covered her hand with his. "I know that." He took a deep breath that was mostly a sigh and gave her his assessment.

Anita relaxed into the back of her chair.

Gordon didn't notice the tilt of her chin or the smile that reached every corner of her face like the rising sun.

"I assure you I will search out the most favorable auctions for each of your pieces. We don't need to sell them as a lot if you can afford to wait for the best opportunities." He looked at her for confirmation.

"This is the most wonderful news," she blurted out.

"What?" It was Gordon's turn to look quizzical.

"I realized while I was walking over here that I don't want to sell them. I love those old machines and the connections I feel with my grandmother and my mother whenever I'm in the basement with them."

"My goodness," were the only words Gordon could muster.

"I enjoy the time I spend taking them apart and refurbishing them." She shrugged. "I guess it's sort of like working a jigsaw puzzle. They're my hobby."

"I can understand that," Gordon said. "I thought that—perhaps—you needed to sell your collection. For your retirement?"

Anita shook her head in answer to his question. "My grandmother left me with a viable business in Archer's Bridals and I inherited the family home when my mother died. It's two blocks that way." She gestured with her thumb behind herself. "It's not a grand old place like the Olsson House, but it's charming and quaint, and suits me to a tee. I don't owe money to anyone and am quite comfortable. The only extra thing I spend money on is travel. I love visiting museums and I've set aside funds to do that."

"The two best things about New York City are Broadway and the museums," said Gordon. "The Met, MOMA, the Whitney, and the Guggenheim are spectacular, but there are dozens of smaller, specialty museums. They're fascinating. Have you been?"

"Once. In college," she said. "Don't laugh, but I was a museum studies major. We took field trips to New York City, Chicago, and Washington, D.C."

"Why would I laugh? I think that's terrific."

"Except I didn't graduate. My mother died unexpectedly, and my grandmother needed help in the shop. I came home. It was supposed to only be for one semester, but one turned into two … you know how that goes."

He nodded. "Did you ever go back?"

She shook her head. "Turns out, I was happy here."

"The dream of being a museum curator is gone?"

She shifted her gaze to the deserted street outside the window. "I think that ship has sailed. I'll satisfy myself with visits to those specialty museums you mentioned."

They sat in silence while the server cleared their plates. They both declined dessert, but accepted cups of coffee.

"If you come to New York, I hope you'll call me. I'd be delighted to be your personal tour guide."

The server delivered their coffee.

"That's awfully kind of you, Gordon." She raised her cup to her lips and blew across the top of the steaming liquid. "Thank you for your time and expertise in evaluating my collection. Now I know I can hang onto it. As I said, that thought makes me surprisingly happy." She took a sip of her coffee. "What do you have planned for the rest of your visit?"

"John is taking the day off tomorrow, and he and I are moving furniture from the attic downstairs. Like you, Maggie has lovely things, but they're not museum quality, so she's going to enjoy them."

"That's wonderful! I can't wait to see them."

"I'm going to help her put them into place on Saturday. That leaves me with a free day on Friday. I thought I'd take a drive through the country and stop at an appliance museum about a hundred miles from here. I discovered it online and it sounds fascinating. Have you been?"

Anita shook her head. "I read about it in the Sunday paper at least a decade ago—and promptly forgot about it." She narrowed her eyes in thought. "Everything in the museum has to fit on a countertop, right? No washers and dryers or anything big?"

"That's right. It's located in an abandoned storefront next to a small hardware store. The owner of the store collected household appliances as a hobby, and, when the men's shop next to him went out of business, he leased the space to house his collection. Apparently, his wife was tired of having them stuffed in every nook and cranny of their home." He tilted his head to his shoulder. "Why don't you do that?"

"Do what?"

"Start a sewing machine museum?"

"In the basement of Archer's?"

"I think you'd need something bigger than that."

"Do you really think people would be interested?"

"I'm sure of it. The reason your collection isn't terribly valuable is because those old machines were indestructible and there were a lot of them made. For most of the twentieth century, every home had a sewing machine. Prices are low because of supply, not demand."

She lowered her cup to the table. "I get at least one call or email a week, asking about restoration. I don't do any advertising about my collection or expertise. My reputation is word-of-mouth."

"Yes!" His hands gesticulated while he talked. "You could offer clinics on sewing machine repair and restoration. Sewing classes. You said yourself there is a need for training in the basics."

She nodded as he continued.

"This would enable you to achieve your lifelong dream of working in a museum."

The smile that had started when he'd told her the collection wasn't valuable now shone with the intensity of noon on a cloudless summer day. "I'm going to have to think about this." She put both hands to the sides of her head. "Maybe you've got something."

He took her hands gently in his, pulling them to the tabletop. "Come with me on Friday. Let's see what this appliance museum is all about."

She looked into his earnest eyes and pushed aside thoughts of fittings and deadlines, accounts payable and inventory to be ordered. "Okay," she said in a breathy voice. "I'd like that."

Gordon released her hands as the waiter approached with their check. "We'll find somewhere wonderful for lunch and make a day of it."

Anita reached for the check, but his longer arms intercepted it.

"Put it on my bill for your services today," Anita said.

"I'll do no such thing," Gordon replied. "And there'll be no charge for today."

"You can't do that! Your time is extremely valuable."

"You're not engaging my services to sell anything. There will be no charge."

She opened her mouth to protest.

"Period," he said, cutting her off. He signed the credit card receipt. "Now, my car is at the curb. I believe you walked here?"

"Yes. My home and the shop are within a few blocks. I never drive to work."

"Then I'll give you a ride home."

"You don't have to do that. Westbury is perfectly safe. I walk in the evenings all the time."

He shook his head. "I understand Westbury isn't New York, but I still can't allow it. My mother would be rolling in her grave if I didn't escort you home."

"We wouldn't want that." Anita smiled at him as he helped her on with her coat and led her to his car.

CHAPTER 27

Alistair:
I sensed the dogs at the entrance to the attic. They shouldn't be on the second floor at this time in the morning.

I'd always prided myself on my sense of time. Maggie had finished her usual weekday routine—coffee, shower, makeup, that blasted noisy hair contraption, clothing, and out the door. John should have preceded her out the door before it even got light outside. I didn't hear him leave.

The door to the attic opened, and I heard John's familiar steps on the stairs, followed by those that I thought belonged to Gordon Mortimer. My suspicion was soon confirmed.

John hoisted a metal contraption in the shape of an L with two wheels onto the attic floor.

"Let's use this dolly to move most of the furniture downstairs. One of us can pull it down step by step while the other keeps it steady," John said.

"Right," Gordon replied. "We'll wrap each piece in a blanket and strap it to the dolly. That way, we won't damage anything. Slow, but steady."

They wrapped a regency accent chest in a blanket and secured it to the dolly. John got in front of it and Gordon took up his position behind it.

Finally! They're moving the furniture downstairs to where it belongs. I followed them down the attic stairs to the main staircase that swept along the wall from the first to the second floors.

They deposited the chest that had been purchased from an English manor home near the base of the stairs.

"Let's bring down all the pieces Maggie said she'd like to use on the first floor," Gordon said, "and put them here. We'll create a staging area on the second floor, too. They'll be out of the way until Maggie and I place them in their permanent positions on Saturday."

"Sounds like a plan," John said.

I looked from the beloved antique to the retreating backs of the men. If I'd heard correctly, my attic was about to become much more spacious. What was the word I'd heard recently on one of the television shows Maggie loved to watch: open plan?

I flitted up and down stairs the entire day as the men wrapped and removed furniture. By the end of the morning, the only pieces remaining were a threadbare old sofa that I considered my easy chair and two massive armoires where I liked to hide when I needed privacy.

John started across the attic toward the armoires.

"Maggie told me this morning she didn't want those," Gordon said.

John dropped onto the sofa. "Thank goodness. We would've needed to hand-carry them. The dolly wouldn't have worked." He picked at the horsehair stuffing protruding from the seat cushions. "This thing is shot."

"You could have it redone," Gordon said.

I held my breath.

"But she said to leave it, as well."

"Our work is done," John said, hoisting himself up. "Let's get out of here."

"I'll bring the dolly with us, in case Maggie and I need it on Saturday," Gordon said.

They left the attic with me at their heels.

I didn't care where the other pieces went, but that regency chest was my favorite. The simplicity of the design allowed the stunning grain pattern to stand out; the brass hardware brought out the gold tones in the wood.

It was the first piece of furniture we encountered at the foot of the stairs. John walked past it, but Gordon lingered.

"This piece has exceptionally pleasing lines," he said.

John turned back to him and studied the piece. "It's handsome, for sure."

I knew where it should go, where it had been placed the moment it had been taken out of its shipping crate, and where it had lived for more than eighty years.

I hovered in front of Gordon, then moved on to John, and went back again. I was uncertain about my telepathic skills, as I had never been given the opportunity to put them to the test. Until now.

TO THE RIGHT OF THE FIREPLACE IN THE LIBRARY, I thought with all my might. Move the fireplace pokers and the potted plant to the other side and place the chest there. I floated between them. *TO THE RIGHT! TO THE RIGHT!*

"You know what?" Gordon looked at John. "Let's place this one piece. If Maggie doesn't like it, we can easily move it. I have the strongest feeling about where it should go."

"Sure," John replied.

I squeezed my eyes shut, afraid to look.

John grasped one end and Gordon took the other.

When I opened my eyes, I knew I'd been right. The regency chest still belonged where they'd put it—to the right of the fireplace in the library.

CHAPTER 28

"Thanksgiving is a week from today," Sunday said as Cara pulled her along, straining at the end of the leash.

"Let's switch dogs," Josh said. Dan walked at his left side, the leash slack between them.

"Cara needs training, doesn't she?" Sunday asked. "I've always had cats, so I guess I don't know how." They exchanged leashes.

"It's easy. Just snap the chain when she pulls ahead and tell her to heel. She's smart—she'll catch on in no time." He demonstrated the technique. "Want to try it?"

Sunday declined. She blew out a breath and watched it crystalize into tiny specks of ice. "It's chilly tonight and supposed to be downright cold next week."

"I like a cold Thanksgiving," Josh said. "Makes it feel like the holidays are coming. Growing up in Atlanta, we often had a sunny day in the sixties. What I'd really love—and have never had—is snow."

They continued on their after-dinner walk and turned the corner onto the next block.

Sunday chuckled. "People from warm climates romanticize snow. All I can think of is icy roads, longer commutes, and scraping my windshield."

"You're right. How about snow on Thanksgiving that melts on the next day?"

"I could go for that." She glanced at him. "What are you doing for Thanksgiving?"

He halted and turned her toward him. Her face was illuminated by a nearby streetlight. His was in darkness.

"You mean what are *we* doing for Thanksgiving? The only thing I'm certain of is that I want to spend the day with you."

Even in the thin light, Josh could see her color rise. "But you have family here now."

"I have Lyla and Robert, but I want you to be my family, too."

Sunday stood in the light, straining to read his expression.

Josh took her in his arms and kissed her, long and slow.

Dan sat patiently at their side, but Cara finally tugged them apart.

"I'd like that," Sunday said in a hoarse whisper.

Josh lost his grasp on Cara's leash. The dog took off across the street, barking frantically.

Josh ran after her, catching up with Cara at the base of a

tree. He snatched up the leash, corrected her, and brought her back to where Sunday and Dan waited.

"She must have seen a squirrel," he said, pausing to rewrap his scarf that had become unwound while he ran.

"Back to Thanksgiving," Sunday said, clearing her throat. Their intimate moment had been broken.

"Lyla has asked us over for dinner, and she and Robert and you and I have been invited to the annual Rosemont potluck. What do you want to do?"

"I've got an idea," Sunday said. "Robert's returning from a London rare book show the morning before. He's going to be jet-lagged and pooped. Lyla told me he didn't want to be part of the large party at Rosemont. She didn't say so, but that's probably why she decided to cook and invite us."

"Makes sense. Thanksgiving is an American holiday, so a Brit like my dad isn't sentimental about it."

"Exactly. I'd like to spend time with them, too."

They walked along, dogs at their sides, at a brisk pace.

"Why don't we host Thanksgiving for Robert and Lyla? We can have it at my house. School shuts down on Wednesday and the library closes at noon. I'll have plenty of time to clean my house and prep the meal."

"We'd be like real grown-ups." Josh smiled at Sunday. "Not just kids who come home for the holiday. I love that idea—on one condition. I get off at noon on Wednesday, too. I'll come over and do all the cleaning. We need to split the expense, too."

"You don't have to..."

He held up his hand to silence her. "It's not up for negotiation. Let's do the grocery shopping together."

"Really?"

"Sure. It's a lot of work to make the list, buy everything, haul it into the house, and put it away."

"You're my dream man! How do you know all this?"

He shrugged.

"Seriously—have you ever hosted a big meal?"

Josh sighed. "Okay—no I haven't. I listen to drive-time radio in the morning and today's call-in topic was hosting Thanksgiving. Most of the callers were women, and they really needed to vent."

"You paid attention. High marks for you!"

Josh looked pleased. "I'll tell Maggie tomorrow that we won't be there."

"Great. Let's FaceTime Robert and Lyla when we get home from our walk to invite *them* for Thanksgiving."

"You're sure she won't be upset? Some of the callers this morning were torqued out about family members derailing their plans."

"I'm positive. Lyla's always gracious, of course. I'm sure her invitation was sincere." They turned at the corner and headed for home. "But she's still recovering from that nasty bout of bronchitis that lasted for weeks. I'm positive she'll jump at the chance to let someone else wrangle the meal this year."

"Good. Then it's settled."

They quickened their pace.

"I'm excited to call them—and for all the fun we'll have doing this," he said.

"Cleaning and shopping are fun?" Sunday asked.

"They are when I'm with you." He inhaled deeply and held his breath before continuing. "We need to continue our discussion about being a family—another time."

Sunday whipped her head around to him, but he was already heading up the walkway to his apartment.

They went inside to place their call.

CHAPTER 29

"What a beautiful day," Anita said.

Gordon opened the passenger door of his car for her.

"Not a cloud in the sky," she continued.

He shut her door and slid into the driver's seat. "They're predicting a storm this weekend—the first snow of the season."

"I saw that on the news. Let's keep an eye on the sky. We don't want to get stuck driving home in a snowstorm." She buckled her seat belt.

"We should be fine, but, just in case, let's start with the museum. We'll have lunch afterward and decide if we'll head directly to Westbury or meander our way back through the country."

"I'm really excited about this," Anita said. "It's so nice of you to include me."

"My pleasure," he replied, smiling over at her.

The ninety-minute drive to their destination flew by, with both of them sharing memories from their childhoods and discussing what they liked—and disliked—in television shows and movies. They shared a passion for British crime dramas, while she favored home improvement shows and he kept up with all major sports.

Gordon followed the navigation program on his phone and parked in front of a hardware store. A sign posted next to the door bore the word "Museum," with an arrow pointing to the east.

They got out of the car and approached a large plate-glass door. The word Museum was painted on the glass in black letters, outlined in gilt. The overhead lights behind the door were off.

"Oh, no," Anita said. "They're closed. I should've called before we came all this way."

"Their website didn't list a closure." Gordon walked up to the door and peered at a 4 x 6 card taped to the door. "It says the museum entrance is through the hardware store, on weekdays."

"Whew! That's a relief."

They entered the hardware store and found a clerk. "You're in luck," the young man said. "The owner's here and the museum is his baby. He'll give you a guided tour, if you'd like."

"That would be wonderful," Gordon said.

The loquacious older man was delighted to take them

through the museum. The small space was neatly arranged by type of appliance, sorted from oldest to newest.

"My main interest is toasters," the man said. "They got me started on all this." He swung his hand around the space. "I repaired my great-grandmother's toaster when I was a boy. The family wanted to get her a new one, but she wouldn't hear of it." He led them to a shelf. "It's the very first appliance in my collection."

"The detailing on it is quite something," Gordon said. "The very best of Art Deco. I don't blame her for wanting to hang onto it."

"That's what I thought—even back then. I've got earlier models." He pointed down the row. "Everything in here is in working order—and none of them sacrificed beauty for utility."

They followed behind him as he expounded on the history and development of mixers, coffee pots, waffle irons, pressure cookers, and bread machines. "I limited my collection to these items when microwaves and food processors hit the scene." He turned to them and chuckled. "Actually, my wife made the decision for me. She told me if I brought one more thing home, I'd have to go." He turned back to his beloved collections. "As you can see, I'm out of space as it is. I miss the thrill of the hunt for new pieces to acquire and restore, but I've got arthritis in my hands and can't do much of that anymore as it is."

Anita touched his arm. "This is a remarkable place," she said. "I've enjoyed our visit so much. I'm glad you were here to give us a tour."

"If you have an interest in any of this, I offer classes on restoration and give talks on collecting. They're quite popular. Where are you from?"

"Westbury," Anita said.

He nodded. "That's a drive, but we've had people come here from as far away as Chicago."

"May I ask you a personal question?" Anita asked.

The man raised an eyebrow.

"Are you happy you opened your museum? Do you find that it's worth the time and effort you put into it?"

His answer came fast. "One thousand percent. I love seeing everything displayed. I can tell you how I acquired each piece in here. And the challenges I encountered restoring it. The best part is the people I meet who share my interest in these beautiful old relics. Young people, old people—and from every walk of life. I've formed friendships with people I'd never have met if I hadn't opened my museum."

He looked around himself. "This museum may be a small offshoot of a hardware store in a tiny town, but it's got a much bigger footprint than you'd imagine. And" —he looked into her eyes— "it makes me happy."

Anita extended her hand to him, and he took it in his. "Thank you. I'm considering opening a sewing machine museum in Westbury," she said. "It's been instructive to see this—and to meet you."

He put his other hand on top of hers and asked a few pertinent questions. When she'd finished her brief description of her collection, he locked eyes with her. "Do it." His voice was resolute. "If you're even half as satisfied as I've been, you'll never regret it."

The man reached into the inside breast pocket of his quilted vest and produced a business card. "I can be a wealth of information for you as you start out. Please call me anytime—for any reason. Who knows—maybe one day we'll do some joint marketing."

Anita pressed the card to her chest. "Thank you so much for your generous offer."

The man walked them to the door. "I hope to hear from you soon," he said, shaking hands with them both.

"My head is spinning," Anita said. She looked at Gordon. "After years of yearning for my dream life, it now seems like it's on the horizon—after only a couple of days. And it's all thanks to you, Gordon." She propelled herself onto her tiptoes and planted a kiss on his cheek as flakes of snow fluttered to the ground around them.

CHAPTER 30

Gordon gripped the steering wheel with both hands as the back end of his car fishtailed on the steep driveway up the hill to Rosemont. His windshield wipers clipped along at full speed but still barely provided sufficient visibility to drive. None of the forecasts had predicted a blizzard. The mile-and-a-half drive from Anita's home had taken him almost fifteen minutes.

The majestic house came into view and his shoulders relaxed for the first time in hours. In hindsight, he was glad the only place to get lunch had been a small sandwich shop across the street from the hardware store and museum. Anita had been anxious about the snow that had begun to fall and insisted they forgo a fancy lunch somewhere else along the way. It had been almost 2 p.m. when they'd left the museum, and they were hungry. They'd consumed their sandwiches and been on their way back to Westbury within twenty minutes.

At first, the snow had been light, and it melted when it hit the highway. He and Anita had engaged in a robust conversation about the museum, with each of them recounting interesting facts and details the other had missed.

Heavy clouds rolled in as the sun set in an early dusk. The winds picked up as they drove into the storm.

They were sixty miles from the first Westbury exit when conditions forced Gordon to reduce his speed to a crawl and he realized the severity of their situation. He'd checked the gas gauge and hoped they'd have enough to get home. The last thing he'd wanted to do was pull off the highway to fill the tank.

He'd tightened his grip and hunched over the steering wheel, concentrating on the triangle of windshield cleared by the wipers. The wind blew snow directly at him like someone was throwing popcorn in his face.

They'd been fine until an accident had narrowed the road to one lane. They'd inched along for thirty minutes until they'd cleared the wreck. With the gas gauge hovering near empty, he'd been forced to pull off the road.

"I'm sorry about this," he'd said to Anita.

"I've been chattering away to distract myself, but I need the restroom," Anita had said. "We're lucky it wasn't us in that accident. I'm impressed with what a skillful driver you are, Gordon. I know this return trip is nerve-wracking."

Her encouragement soothed his fraying nerves. She returned to the car after her trip to the ladies' room with large cups of coffee, hotdogs from a rotating display, and two kinds of potato chips. "Dinner," Anita said as she handed him a hot dog. "It's not much, but these are the last two they had. Bon appétit."

He wolfed down his as they drove along the frontage road to the freeway entrance. "I can't believe I'm saying this, but that's a delicious hot dog," he remarked as he swallowed the last bite.

Anita chuckled. "I was thinking the same thing. I don't know if it's the circumstances" —she pointed out the window— "or if they're really that good. We'll have to come back another time—for dinner—to check it out."

Gordon reprised his death grip on the wheel, and they'd continued their journey. Anita had kept up a patter of light conversation and passed him a handful of chips or his cup of coffee whenever he'd asked for them.

Gordon had turned onto her unplowed street shortly after eleven. He started to turn the wheels to the curb when Anita stopped him.

"Stop in the middle of the street," she said. "Nobody else is out in this mess. It's already drifting. If you turn in, you might get stuck."

He stopped the car and unbuckled his seat belt.

Anita put her hand on his elbow and turned him toward her. "You are *not* getting out and walking me to my door. I'm more than capable of seeing myself inside. Rules of gentlemanly behavior are suspended during a snow emergency."

He pursed his lips and nodded at her. "I guess that's practical."

She unbuckled her seat belt and opened her door. "I've had a wonderful day, Gordon. Thank you for planning it. I hope we stay in touch. Have a safe trip home."

He leaned toward her, but she was already outside and closing her door. Gordon sat and watched her until her front door opened. She had turned toward his car, idling in the road, and waved before stepping inside.

Now that he was safe at Rosemont, fatigue washed over Gordon like a palpable force. He pulled around the side of the house to the garage. Six-foot-high drifts already obscured the doors. He steered into an area that he thought was paved and not grass and shut off the engine.

His hands felt welded to the steering wheel. He finally pried them away. He'd texted Maggie and John with an update on their progress home while they'd been getting gas. John had replied with the back-door code and the alarm code so he could get in if they were in bed. Maggie had texted that she'd left a bowl of homemade chicken noodle soup in the refrigerator and crackers on the countertop for his supper. He was to help himself to sourdough toast.

Gordon brushed his hand across his eyes. This is what it was like to have people who genuinely cared for him. He opened John's text and made his way into the house that now felt like home.

CHAPTER 31

The stripe of sunlight emanating from a break in the heavy draperies moved across the bed as the morning wore on until it lay across Pam's face. She snuggled against her sleeping husband and opened one eye. They'd been so exhausted by the grueling final hours of the drive the night before that they'd unloaded their car, given Chance a comfort break, and fallen into the bed of their vacation rental without taking off anything other than their coats and boots.

She lifted her head from the pillow and searched the floor until she found their dog. Chance was curled into a ball on the hearthrug, dead to the world. He usually was the first one up in the morning, eager to relieve himself outside and hurry in for his breakfast. The drive must have taken it out of him, too, she thought.

Pam rolled onto her back and maneuvered out from under Steve's outstretched arm.

His hand landed on the mattress and he woke with a start. He reached for her as she moved to the side of the bed and pulled her back to him. "Are you sure you want to get up?"

Pam looped her arms around his neck. "I guess that depends. What do you have in mind?"

Steve ran a series of kisses down her neck. "This is our official honeymoon, right?"

"That's the idea."

"I suggest we get out of these clothes, for starters." He tore his sweatshirt over his head and sent it sailing across the room before doing the same with Pam's sweater.

"We're overdressed in these jeans," she replied, her voice husky.

The stripe of sunlight continued its course across the bed as Pam and Steve expressed their love for each other. They were lying on their backs, spent and satisfied, when Chance leapt onto the foot of the bed.

"Hey, buddy," Steve said, patting the fluffy comforter on the bed between Pam and himself, beckoning for the dog to join them.

Chance remained on his feet, stepping from side to side, and barked while glancing to the door.

"He's got to go out," Pam said, throwing back the covers.

"I'll take him," Steve said, lowering his feet to the floor and searching until he found his pants and shoes. "I want to see how much more snow came down last night after we arrived."

Pam got to her feet and lunged for her jacket. "It's freezing in here."

"I'll make a fire as soon as we're back inside. The listing said the stone fireplace heats the entire cabin."

Chance raced to the door.

Pam pulled on her jeans. "I hope so, or I'm going to spend our honeymoon in enough layers to look like the Michelin Man."

"You'll be the sexiest Michelin Man on the planet," he said with a lascivious grin. "I'm certain I'd enjoy unwrapping you."

Chance whined.

"Go on," Pam said. "I'll set up breakfast in bed."

Steve opened the front door and faced a three-foot-high wall of snow. He kicked at the drift until Chance jumped onto it and made his way toward a post that held up the porch roof.

The dog lifted his leg. Steve was about to admonish him about discoloring the snow on the porch when he realized he didn't know where the steps to the porch were located. The landscape was blanketed with snow. Drifts were deep against the house and undulated like sand dunes until they met the forest that surrounded the property. Snow sat high on bare branches. The SUV was buried to the tops of its tires.

The wind had died down and snow was still falling, but not with the vengeance of the previous night. Streaks of blue sky punctuated the clouds, and the sun made the surface of the snow glitter like a blanket of diamonds.

He inhaled the cold, clear air until the insides of his nose froze.

Chance gazed out at the same vista, then looked at Steve as he wagged his tail.

"You want to play in the snow, don't you, boy?"

Chance uttered a single "Woof," then tore off the porch, his legs pumping like pistons in the deep snow. He bounded to the right, then swung in the opposite direction and buried his snout. He raised his nose, sneezed, and then buried it again. Chance dug, his paws sending pellets of snow flying in every direction.

"What're you doing? It's time for breakfast. At least for you," he muttered under his breath.

Chance shoved his nose deeper into the snow and came up with a tennis ball. He high-stepped back to Steve and deposited the ball at his master's feet.

"Look what you found!" Steve reached down and picked up the ball. "We'll come out later, with Pam, to play fetch. We'll also need to find a snow shovel. I assume they have one."

The dog looked up at him and wagged his tail.

"Being snowed in for a day will be fun, but we'll eventually have to dig out."

They opened the door and were greeted with a warm blast of air.

"This place has central heating," Pam said. She was sitting in bed, her knees drawn up in front of her. A tray sat in the middle of the bed, loaded with sleeves of white powdered-sugar donuts, cinnamon-y bear claws, three bananas, and two steaming cups of coffee. "I found the thermostat. I'd still love you to make a fire. It'll be so cozy."

"I'll feed him first," Steve said.

Pam shook her head. "I've got his bowl with kibble right here." She pointed to Chance's bowl placed next to the tray.

Steve raised an eyebrow.

"If we're having breakfast in bed, so is he." She patted the bed and Chance needed no further invitation. He crunched his kibble with characteristic relish.

Steve found the matches that the host stored on the mantel and lit the fire that had already been laid. The flames caught on the kindling and the logs soon succumbed.

"Is this what you bought while we were getting gas the last time?" He admired the spread on the tray.

She nodded. "There wasn't much to choose from. People had the same idea I had—to stock up."

"I'm starved," he said. "This looks delicious to me." He toed off his snowy boots and climbed under the covers.

She handed him his coffee. "If you think this looks good, wait until you see lunch and dinner."

He popped a donut into his mouth and ate it in one bite. "What's on the menu?"

"Luncheon will consist of beef jerky, potato chips, and bean dip."

"What's wrong with that? I used to have that all the time—before I married such a wonderful cook."

"Dinner will be Italian. I bought the last two cans of

SpaghettiOs within a hundred miles, a box of Cheez-Its, and red Gatorade that we can pretend is wine."

He held his palms up toward the ceiling. "Another favorite. What's for dessert?"

Pam slanted her eyes at him. "I guarantee you'll love what I've got planned for dessert."

CHAPTER 32

Maggie wiped the dust off the top of the pedestal table she and John had moved from the foyer to the conservatory to make way for the one John and Gordon had brought down from the attic. "There," she said, stepping back. "It looks terrific in here. Let's move the replacement table into the foyer and then I'll make lunch."

John leaned back, both hands at the small of his back, and stretched. "What about that large secretary?"

"That's too much for the two of us to handle. We'll wait until Gordon gets up."

They retraced their steps and soon had the Victorian table of walnut-burled wood in position. Gold leaf accented the carved flowers that circled the top, and an inlaid center design in a golden swirl made the piece a stunner with no additional decoration.

She slipped her arm around her husband's waist as they stood, admiring the table.

"That's absolutely gorgeous." They turned to find Gordon stepping off the bottom step. "I'll bet they purchased it to go right there," he said.

"Good morning," Maggie said. "Why do you think it was ever banished to the attic?"

Gordon shrugged. "Who knows? Sometimes people simply want a change."

"I'm so glad you encouraged us to move these lovely pieces into our living spaces. That table" —she gestured to it with her head— "is never going anywhere else. Not while I'm living here."

"I'm glad to hear it." Gordon looked around himself. "I see the secretary, but where's everything else?"

"I came across Maggie moving one of the small end tables after breakfast. I offered to help." John chuckled. "The next thing I knew, it was lunchtime, and we had moved everything except the secretary. I'd say I've been Tom Sawyered."

Maggie cuffed his arm playfully. "I was fine on my own. You didn't need to help me."

Gordon smoothed his hair with his hand. "I should have been down here to help. I'm sorry I slept so late."

"Not at all," John said. "I woke briefly when you got in. That means you drove at least ten hours yesterday, most of it in a blizzard. Anyone would be exhausted. Besides, the new vet at Westbury Animal Hospital opened up this morning and called to say that all but two of our appointments canceled because of the weather. I had an unexpected day off."

"I hope we didn't make so much noise that we woke you," Maggie said.

"Not at all. I guess you're right, John. I haven't slept this late in decades."

"You must be starved," Maggie said.

As if on cue, Gordon's stomach rumbled. "That soup you left for me was delicious, Maggie. The drive *was* stressful. The soup calmed my nerves and helped me get to sleep."

"I'll go put lunch on the table. We're having snow day food."

Gordon lifted an eyebrow.

"When I was little, my mother always made macaroni and cheese when school was canceled. We'd have it with apple slices and buttered bread."

"That sounds delightful," Gordon said. "After lunch, will you show me where you've placed all the pieces? I'd love to see them in their new homes."

"Yes. If you think there are better places for them, please speak up. I haven't decorated any of them, so I'd appreciate your suggestions on that, too."

"I'd be more than happy to, Maggie. You've got plenty of fine, decorative objects on display at Rosemont. I suggest we 'shop the house' to style these pieces."

Maggie clasped her hands together. "I love the sound of that."

"Do you know where you want the secretary?" Gordon asked.

She shook her head no.

"I've got an idea."

"Surprise me," Maggie said, heading for the kitchen. "I can't wait for our Thanksgiving guests to see the changes we've made."

～

Maggie spooned fragrant servings of macaroni, dripping with melted cheese, from a Crock-pot on the kitchen island. She handed one bowl to Gordon and one to John. "A pitcher of iced tea is on the kitchen table, along with a plate of sliced apples and a basket of warm bread."

They sat together and tucked into the comfort food.

"This meal makes the horror of that drive worth it," Gordon said.

"I wouldn't go that far," Maggie said, "but I'm glad you're enjoying it."

Gordon glanced out the window in the breakfast room. "It's still snowing, but the wind has died down and it's not accumulating so fast."

"I've checked my weather apps," John said. "This is the tail end of the storm. Snow is supposed to stop by dinner time. The plows will have the roads in town open by the morning."

"That's good," Gordon began before John cut him off.

"We don't think you should leave tomorrow." He looked at Maggie and she nodded her agreement. "The storm is crawling to the east and dropping record snowfall. You'd be driving into it the entire way home."

"I had the radio on while I was getting dressed and heard the same thing."

Maggie tilted her head toward her shoulder. "I know you've got engagements in the city next week, but, if the blizzard hits New York on Monday, as predicted, won't those get canceled?"

"My assistant has already emailed me to that effect."

Maggie leaned over the table toward him. Her eyes gleamed. "Then you have no reason to hurry back. Please stay here and join us for Thanksgiving."

"An unexpected houseguest for a holiday is …"

Maggie slapped the table. "I'm not listening to one more word of that," she said. "You'd be doing us a favor, in fact. Besides helping me decorate the furniture we've hauled downstairs, we can set the tables this afternoon."

"I'd be more than happy to …"

"I'm not done," Maggie said. "As I told you when we spoke several weeks ago, John puts up a gazillion Christmas lights, and everyone steps outside at dusk after Thanksgiving dinner to see them light up for the first time. He's usually done by the weekend before the holiday, but he got behind when we extended our trip to Linden Falls. He planned to get caught up this weekend." She opened her palms to the ceiling and shrugged. "And now this."

"Maggie's right. I called every handyman I know when we got home from vacation, but they're all busy—except for our friend Joe Torres. If we hadn't been snowed in this weekend, we might have finished it. I'd resigned myself to having a smaller display this year, but if you stay to lend a hand … well …"

Gordon swallowed a growing lump in his throat. There was nowhere he'd rather be on Thanksgiving than right here, at Rosemont. "You're sure?"

"Yes!" they both responded.

"Then I'd be delighted to stay, and you can count on me for any task you care to assign—from outside light stringer to scullery maid."

Maggie leapt to her feet and began clearing their dishes. "We're going to have so much fun. I can't wait to show you the lovely fall-themed table linens I bought at a farmers market in Vermont. You'll appreciate the craftsmanship."

John took the dishes from her hands. "The two of you can get started. I'll finish up here and then I'm headed to the library to do paperwork."

Gordon stood and picked up his bowl and cutlery. "Allow me. I don't want to delay you from your paperwork."

"'Going to the library to do paperwork' is code for John's settling into the sofa, turning the television to something sports-related, and taking a long nap." Maggie leaned in to kiss her husband's cheek. "And as hard as he works, I'm thrilled when he gets the chance to be a couch potato."

Gordon looked between the happy couple and felt a visceral pull on his heartstrings. His parents had had such a connection, and he had wanted one for himself, too. A surge of sadness coursed through him as he wondered when he'd given up on the idea.

CHAPTER 33

Pam wound her scarf around her neck and slung her purse over her shoulder.

Steve waited by the front door, Chance at his feet. "I'm glad the local radio station says the roads are open this morning. We didn't starve yesterday—thanks to your foresight at the convenience store when we gassed up—but I'm starving now. The Mill is supposed to have a killer Sunday brunch, but they don't allow dogs except for legitimate service animals." He looked into the brown eyes trained on him. "Which this guy is not."

"I'm sure we'll find someplace wonderful in town." Pam picked up a brown tin tied with an orange ribbon. "Do you mind if we run by Rosemont today? I want to leave this tin of troll cookies and our thank you note to Maggie and John by their front door."

"It's a good thing I forgot we had those," Steve said. "I would have devoured them in the middle of the night."

Pam gave him a side eye as she stepped past him and the dog onto the porch. "That would have been the fastest way to end this honeymoon—and possibly this marriage."

"Aren't you taking those cookies a bit *too* seriously?"

"Mom and I baked and decorated two batches until we got them to look like pilgrims and Indians for Thanksgiving." She lifted the tin. "These are the best of both batches. I wanted to give them something I'm proud of. Maggie and John gave us a piece of heirloom silver, for heaven's sake. That's remarkably kind of them. And that throw was over the top."

He locked the door behind them. "I agree," he said. "I just wish we'd brought some cookies for us."

"You ate them all before we left Linden Falls." She pulled down her sunglasses to look at him.

"I guess I did."

They crossed the frozen ground and got into the car.

"Do we eat, or deliver the cookies and thank you note first?"

Pam pulled up a map of Westbury on her phone. "Rosemont is about here." She pointed to a spot on her screen. "And the square with shops and restaurants is about a mile further on. Let's drop these off first and then find a place for breakfast. It's early, so we can probably sneak in and out of Rosemont without anyone seeing us."

"Sounds like a plan." Steve steered their car out of their snowy driveway and onto the clear pavement of a state road.

Pam input Rosemont's address into her phone's navigation app, and within fifteen minutes they were climbing the winding driveway to the house.

"They've already had their drive plowed," Steve remarked. "I'm impressed."

"You can see a bunch of stone chimneys over the treetops," Pam said in a breathless voice.

They both gasped as they rounded a corner and the elegant, stone manor home came into full view. Mullioned windows reflected the warm glow of the morning sun. Unblemished snow coated the roof like a layer of vanilla frosting. Icicles dripped from the eves.

Pam removed her sunglasses and tossed them on the dashboard. "I've seen photos online, but they don't do this justice."

"It's pretty incredible." Steve stopped the car across from the front door.

Pam grabbed the tin and card, and got out of the car. Steve joined her, leaving his car door ajar.

They slowly mounted the stone steps leading to the front door, swiveling their heads from side to side to take in every detail. A polished brass lion's head knocker adorned the massive mahogany door that curved along the top in a graceful arch. Pam set their tin of cookies on the mat, then repositioned it to lean up against the door.

They were looking up, examining the ornate iron light fixture hanging on the porch, when an insistent round of barking broke the silence of the peaceful scene. Pam and

Steve glanced at each other. The commotion came from more than one dog—and they recognized Chance's bark.

Steve tore down the stairs two steps at a time, with Pam at his heels. They followed the noise to the right and around the side of the house.

Chance and a golden retriever were wrestling, barking up a storm, and wagging their tails at warp speed. John Allen was walking toward them, a ladder balanced on his shoulder. A tall, thin man they didn't recognize followed John carrying an open, plastic tote with strings of Christmas lights spilling out the top.

"Steve!" John set the ladder on the ground. "Pam." He raced to them, his arms extended.

Pam slipped into his embrace, and they hugged. "For a minute, I thought I was seeing things," John said as he shook Steve's hand.

"Who's this guy?" John pointed at Chance.

"That's our dog—Chance," Steve said before calling to his dog.

Chance turned to his master briefly, then continued playing with Roman.

Steve moved to corral his dog.

"Leave him," John said. "They're having fun. What are you both doing here?"

"That's a long story." Pam drew in a deep breath before she began.

"No." John held up a hand. "Maggie's going to want to hear all of it." He turned to Gordon. "We've got introductions to make, too. Let's go inside. Maggie's in the kitchen."

Without waiting for a response, John led them inside.

Maggie was removing an egg strata casserole from the oven, its cheesy top bubbly and browned. Freshly baked cinnamon rolls cooled on a rack on the counter.

"Look who I found loitering out front," John said.

She looked up, and her surprised expression instantly turned to delight.

"Are my eyes deceiving me?" She swept the newlyweds into a group hug.

"We were dropping off our thank you note," Pam said. "We don't want to disturb you."

"What in the world are you doing in Westbury?" Maggie asked, taking a step back but holding onto their arms. "You didn't come all the way from Vermont to do that."

"No," Pam said. "I'm not sure where to begin …"

"I do," Maggie said. "Let's start with breakfast. Everything's fresh out of the oven and we have more than enough. That's what happens when we're snowed in: I make lots and lots of food."

"We shouldn't impose," Steve began.

"You'd be doing no such thing," John said. "First, let me introduce our friend, Gordon Mortimer."

Following introductions—including of the dogs who raced inside after them, tracking wet footprints across the kitchen floor—they each helped themselves and sat at the kitchen table for the meal. Pam and Steve brought them up to date on the happenings in Linden Falls after Maggie and John left and recounted the tale of their treacherous drive two days before.

"These are the best cinnamon rolls I've ever had," Steve said when he'd finished talking, licking icing from his fingers.

Maggie got up and brought the pan to the table. "Have another one," she said. "After yesterday, you both deserve seconds."

Pam and Steve looked at each other and helped themselves to a second roll.

"I'm so happy you got Chance back. The story of how he found you at your wedding" —she wiped the lingering dampness from beneath her eyes— "belongs in a novel. Or in a Hallmark movie."

"Thank you," Pam said. "You don't think we're overreacting by bringing him on our honeymoon?"

"Not at all," Maggie, John, and Gordon said in unison.

John drained his coffee cup and got to his feet. "I hate to interrupt this, but Gordon and I have lights to put on the house before Thursday."

Gordon followed suit, and they exited through the kitchen door.

"We'll get out of your hair," Steve said, rising and picking up plates from the table.

"Leave the dishes," Maggie commanded. "You'll have a lot of fun exploring the square today. It's almost noon, and that's when the shops open. Would you like a tour of Rosemont before you go? I know you host that home improvement show on television, so you're interested in houses."

"I'd adore that," Pam said.

Steve nodded his agreement.

"I'll give you the complete tour, on one condition."

They looked at her with raised eyebrows.

"The two of you join us for Thanksgiving."

"I don't know," Pam began. "We've already barged in for breakfast."

"You didn't barge in—you were invited. As I said earlier, it's a potluck and everyone comes. The meal is fabulous, and we have the best time after dinner playing games and singing Christmas carols." She narrowed her eyes. "Now that I think of it, our Thanksgiving is a modern-day version of the original. Anyway—it would make my day if you'd come. I've already told my daughter and our friends about the two of you. They'll be delighted to meet you."

Pam and Steve looked at each other, then grinned.

"We'll be there," Steve said.

"Thank you," Pam added. "What should we bring?"

"Eggnog," Maggie said. "We ran out last year. Everyone wants it after they come in from seeing the lights. A carton of eggnog will do nicely."

"We'll bring two," Steve said.

"And now," Maggie said, "let's start our tour at the back door. To the left is the original butler's pantry …"

CHAPTER 34

Alistair:

My goodness, things have been busy around here for a Sunday. First, there was that nice young couple Maggie led through the entire house. They were so interested in everything that Maggie even took them up to my attic. I wasn't expecting that.

The woman called Pam zeroed in on the barrel of dishes right away. She admired them, being extra careful with the plate Maggie handed her to examine. I approved.

I trailed downstairs after them as Maggie bid them goodbye at the front door.

Pam picked up a gift from the doormat and handed it to Maggie.

I hovered over her shoulder as Maggie opened it and hit my head on the hanging fixture when I recoiled in shock.

Those were the weirdest-looking pilgrims I'd ever seen. What were they teaching in the schools these days?

Maggie laughed as she examined each cookie, complimenting Pam on her skill and creativity.

Pam blushed and deflected Maggie's praise with self-effacing comments. I liked the young woman, so I forgave her for her shocking lack of knowledge about pilgrims.

The man emitted a high-pitched whistle as he and Pam walked to their car. An enormous black dog bounded up to them. I sank into the shadows on the porch. Dogs are always able to detect me, even when humans can't.

The dog looked my way, then launched himself into the back seat at his master's command. The couple and their dog drove away.

John and Gordon were working at the far end of the house. Gordon was standing at the top of our tallest ladder, securing icicle lights to hooks attached to the eaves. John was untangling the strings of lights and handing them to Gordon. I'd seen John do this in prior years. The two of them were making fast work of it.

Roman raced through the snow on the front lawn. The beautiful, unblemished blanket was now crisscrossed with paw prints. He flopped onto his back and wriggled like he does when John rubs his belly. Roman was a good dog, and I was happy he was enjoying himself in the snow, even if he was messing up the view from the attic windows.

I decided to inspect the men's efforts and floated toward them.

Gordon climbed down the ladder and moved it to a

spot five feet over. He put his right foot on the bottom rung and was about to scale it again when his thin rectangular box with the glass screen—which I recently learned is called a cell phone—rang. It announced the caller as Anita Archer.

I stopped in my tracks. In my day, I answered the telephone and announced callers. The master or mistress of the house would decide if they wanted to accept the call. I knew them so well, I could predict which ones they would answer and which callers I would supply with a plausible excuse when I returned to the line.

The modern world had replaced me with a thin, black box. If the recipient didn't want to speak with the caller, there wasn't a real person to convey information or let the caller down cordially. I didn't call this progress.

"Do you mind if I take this?" Gordon asked John as he raised the phone to his ear.

John nodded. "Of course. I'll bring more totes of lights from the garage." He walked off to give Gordon some privacy.

I moved in closer—until I could hear both ends of the conversation.

"I just called to wish you a safe drive home and to thank you, again, for coming up with the idea for my museum. I spent the entire day yesterday researching online and making plans. My list is a mile long. And I owe it all to you."

I was close enough to feel the heat rise from Gordon's collar as he flushed at her kind words.

"How are the roads?" Anita continued. "The weather

reports show you'll be driving into the storm by the afternoon."

"I saw that," Gordon replied. "Maggie and John were kind enough to insist that I stay on at Rosemont rather than get into that mess."

"That's wonderful news! I was hoping you'd delayed your departure."

"I'm staying through Thanksgiving, actually. John and I are putting up Christmas lights at the moment. I'll help Maggie set up and prepare the meal, too."

"I'm sure they appreciate the help."

"Will I see you—at Thanksgiving?" he asked. "Maggie's told me it's a huge potluck and everyone comes."

"You will—I wouldn't miss it for the world. Maybe we'll run into each other before Thursday."

"I'd like that. I'd planned to call you this evening to invite you to dinner one night."

"I've got a better idea," Anita said. "Come to my house for dinner—tonight."

Gordon's pink neck was now beet red.

"I don't want to put you to any trouble. Shall we go out?"

"I'd like to treat you to dinner as a thank you for everything you've done for me, but you won't let me pick up the check."

"It's how I was raised."

"Then I guess you're going to have to come to my house. You don't need to be afraid. I'm a decent cook. Ask Maggie."

"I'm sure you are," Gordon stammered.

"It's settled. See you at six. After yesterday's storm, I'm

hankering for comfort food. I'll make a pot roast with all the fixings."

"That sounds wonderful. See you then. And thank you."

He tapped the screen, and her voice was gone. Gordon stared into the distance, and I recognized the look of a love-struck school boy.

John reappeared with another large plastic box overflowing with lights.

"You okay, Gordon?" he asked.

Gordon swung to him. "Yes. Fine." He cleared his throat. "Would you and Maggie mind if I went out for dinner tonight?"

John set the tote on the ground. "With Anita?"

Gordon nodded. "She's invited me to her home for a meal."

"Lucky you," John said. "Next to my wife, she's the best home cook in town."

Gordon grinned. "Should I take her flowers?"

"If a man asks if he should take flowers to a woman, the answer is always yes." John looked at his friend. "The florists are closed on Sunday, but the grocery stores have nice floral departments."

Gordon rubbed his hands together. "Right. That's what I'll do."

"Let's put up lights until four. It starts to get dark around four-thirty, anyway. That'll give you plenty of time to clean up, buy your flowers, and get to Anita's."

Gordon propelled himself to the top of the ladder at top

speed. "We're making terrific progress. With any luck, we'll finish by then."

My, my. Gordon has a romantic interest. I supposed I'd seen Anita Archer at a recent Thanksgiving, but I couldn't place her. I remembered her great-grandmother and grandmother. They were both kind and beautiful women. For Gordon's sake, I hoped she took after her ancestors.

The bright sunshine belied the frigid temperature. I shivered and decided to head inside and check on Maggie and my little friend Eve.

CHAPTER 35

Josh checked his work email. Nothing new had come in for the last forty-five minutes. Things had been slow all day on this Tuesday before Thanksgiving. No one had called Maggie since before lunch.

He turned back to his personal laptop and read the email again. He was being offered a position in the financial aid office of a major university three hours from Westbury. The school was prestigious, the salary more than competitive, and it was one rung above entry level. He wasn't particularly interested in financial aid, but the job would be impressive on his resume. He could stay in the position for a couple of years and then move on. A year ago, he would've been overjoyed by the offer and snapped it up.

This wasn't a year ago—it was now. He was deeply in love with Sunday and thrilled to be reunited with Robert and

Lyla, all of whom lived in Westbury. He wanted to stay here, too.

Maggie's office door opened, and the university president headed across the reception area, coffee cup in hand. "We're so quiet this afternoon. I'm having trouble staying awake." She held up her coffee cup. "This is my third cup of the day."

"Why don't you head home early? I'll call if anything comes up," he said.

Maggie filled her cup and walked over to his desk. "I was going to say the same to you. Since you and Sunday are hosting at her place, I'm sure you have things to do."

"It's only the four of us. We'll manage. You're having a big crowd."

"Gordon's been the most tremendous help. After working with John to finish the outside lights, he polished silver, ironed tablecloths, and set the tables. Following a brief lesson on knife skills, he even chopped the celery, carrots, and onion for the stuffing. I'm ready. I don't mind holding down the fort for once." She studied his face. "Something's bothering you. Is everything all right?"

Josh closed his laptop. "I'm just busy," he lied. "End of semester exams and papers."

"Hmmm …" Maggie continued to scrutinize him. "All the more reason to get out of here. Study, get ready for Thursday, take a nap—it's up to you. Make sure you do something to alleviate stress. I feel it pouring off of you."

Josh rose, pulling his jacket off the back of his chair. "Don't worry about me." He forced a smile as he donned the jacket. "Everything will be fine." He wasn't lying to his boss.

If worse came to worse, he'd take the job in financial aid and commute to Westbury every weekend. People made long-distance relationships work all the time. Hadn't Sunday already hinted at that very thing to him?

"I know you and Sunday are having a cozy meal with your parents. That's super nice. I remember how excited I was to host my first Thanksgiving. The turkey and stuffing were perfect, but I forgot a pecan pie in the oven, and it was blackened before blackened became a thing. Even so, I was proud of my efforts. You will be, too."

"Thank you. Sunday's nervous. She's printed out a spreadsheet with tasks assigned in fifteen-minute blocks until we sit down at the table. That's the last entry." He smiled and shook his head as he put his laptop in his backpack. "I think that's a bit much."

"Word of advice?" Maggie set her mug on the desk. "Don't mention that to her. I use a typed timeline, too. It keeps me organized and frees my brain, so I don't have to be constantly focused on what needs to be done. I look at my list and do it. John used to tease me about it and that irritated me. I felt belittled and patronized."

Josh took a step back. "Geez. Has John stopped … talking to you about it?"

"He sure has. And we're both happier for it."

"Good to know," Josh said. "Once we sit down to eat, the obsessing should be over with."

"Exactly. And since we're talking about things being more relaxed once dinner is finished, why don't all four of you come to Rosemont afterward for coffee, games, and the annual carol sing? We'd love to have you. There will be plenty of people there your age—including the young couple I told you about from Linden Falls. I think you'll really enjoy each other."

"Thank you. What time?"

"It makes no difference. Come when you can."

"I'll suggest it to the others." He crossed to the reception room door. "Thanks again for letting me knock off before quitting time."

"You're welcome," she said. "And if you pull a Maggie and leave your pie in the oven, join us for dessert. We always have more than enough."

CHAPTER 36

John and Gordon stepped through the back door into the kitchen.

Eve and Roman greeted them effusively.

"We smelled the roasting turkeys from the garage," John called to Maggie in the kitchen. He scratched his beloved golden retriever behind the ears. "Is that why you abandoned us today, Roman?" He held the dog's muzzle and looked into his brown eyes. "I don't blame you. It's so overpowering you can practically taste it."

Roman thumped his tail against the floor.

Gordon bent and ran his hands along Eve's back. The small terrier mix kissed his chin in appreciation.

All four entered the kitchen to find Maggie checking the thermometer inserted into a turkey roasting in the lower wall oven.

"They're done," she said, switching off the oven. She

removed the roasting pan and placed it on the counter, next to three countertop roasters. All three were without their lids. "They need to rest for thirty minutes, and then you can carve them."

Gordon walked along the row of roast turkeys, admiring their shiny, crisp, brown skin. Clear juices oozed from under the skin and into the pans. "These are the largest birds I've ever seen in person," he said.

"Each of them is between thirty-two and thirty-four pounds." Maggie tucked an errant strand of hair behind her ear.

"I've heard people stress over cooking one turkey." He caught Maggie's eyes. "And here you've done four of them."

Maggie grinned at him. "It's not that much more work to do four than one. I'd rather do this than make the side dishes and get everything to the table hot and fresh at one time."

"That's understandable."

"The only additional thing I contribute is stuffing. You helped me make that. The pans are staying warm in the upper oven."

"Do you know what we traditionally do around here while the turkeys rest?" John asked.

Gordon shook his head.

"We go into the library and put our feet up until our guests arrive. While the turkeys rest, we do the same."

"That's wise."

John whistled for Roman to follow him. "He's well-trained, but I'm not leaving this guy alone with four Thanksgiving turkeys. He's tall enough to grab one off the counter."

Gordon chuckled. "Who could blame him?"

Maggie trailed after them, with Gordon bringing up the rear. She paused in the arched entryway to the dining room and flipped the switch for the massive chandelier. Dozens of cut-glass crystals sent rainbows ricocheting around the walls. Silver sparkled and china gleamed. "You've set everything up beautifully, Gordon. You have a wonderful eye for decor." She pulled her phone out of her apron pocket. "I took pictures so I could recreate this next year. Unless we can persuade you to come back?" She peered at him over the top of her reading glasses.

"You're too kind. I simply placed things here and there. Those linens you purchased on your vacation are lovely. They brought the right amount of color and texture into the tablescape without overpowering it."

"As if polishing the silver and setting the tables wasn't enough," Maggie said, "you brought those antique dishes we found in the attic downstairs, washed them, and put them to use."

"The rust, peach, and plum tones in the pattern mix perfectly with the linens. And the intricate swirl pattern of the gold-plated rims—well—they're stunning. If you don't use these dishes at Thanksgiving, when would you ever do so?"

Maggie nodded. "I'm glad you've encouraged me to use and enjoy our beautiful things."

"Exactly."

"I'm excited to show them to Susan, Joan Torres, and Judy Young. You remember meeting them?"

He nodded.

"They're going to flip when they enter this room."

"You guys coming?" John called from the library. "If you don't sit down now, you'll lose your chance."

"John's right," Maggie said, turning away from the dining room with one last admiring glance. "I love the time right before a party starts." They walked across the living room and entered the library. "When everything is ready, and you have a few moments to catch your breath."

"You're expecting forty, more or less?" Gordon asked. "That's the number of places I set at the various tables."

Maggie nodded. She crossed to the small drop-leaf table they'd hauled down from the attic and set in front of the fireplace. With the leaves extended, it seated four comfortably and six if everyone squished in.

"This is the coziest seating in the house," Maggie said. "Let's leave this where it is all weekend and eat in here. I have to warn you," she spoke to Gordon. "I make four turkeys so that I have plenty of leftovers. Every meal from here on out will be something from the fridge that's warmed up."

"Duly noted," he replied, "and good thinking."

Maggie sank onto the sofa next to John while Gordon settled into a wing chair that had been moved away from the fireplace to make room for the table.

They'd barely gotten comfortable when Roman and Eve raced to the front door, barking like mad.

"That'll be Sam and Joan Torres," John said. "They're dear friends. Sam is also the best handyman in town. They arrive early so Sam can double-check that the outdoor lights work.

He always finds something that needs fixing, but I don't think he will this year." John smiled at Gordon. "I think we've nailed it."

"Joan makes the gravy. She uses the juices from the turkeys and the broth I made with the necks and giblets." Maggie hoisted herself from her seat with an involuntary groan. "Everyone raves about her gravy, and I agree with them. I've never found a stray lump of flour."

Gordon followed them to the door. "Your family and friends Thanksgiving tradition is," his voice grew husky, "remarkable."

"We want you to come back next year and make it your tradition, too, Gordon." John placed his hand on Gordon's shoulder and gave it a squeeze.

Gordon swallowed the growing lump in his throat. He'd been invited back by both of them. Maggie and John considered him part of their inner circle, and that made him thankful.

CHAPTER 37

*R*oman, Eve, and Chance paced in the screened-in porch that opened off the back door and ran along the outside of the breakfast room. They pressed their noses to the glass windows that allowed them to view the kitchen and the festivities beyond whenever someone new entered the scene. John had confined them to the porch while food was laid out on every surface, telling them they'd be invited inside for the after-dinner activities.

John and Sam finished carving the turkeys and arranged the slices of juicy white and dark meat on enormous china turkey platters. Joan's gravy simmered on the stove, ready to be ladled onto food right from the pot.

Guests milled about, exchanging greetings and engaging in small talk. A green salad, homemade cranberry relish, and rolls and butter in the shape of a turkey were positioned at one end of the kitchen island. Next came Crock-pots of macaroni and cheese, mashed potatoes, two kinds of sweet potato casserole, stuffing, and green beans—both steamed and baked in the traditional mushroom soup casserole topped with onion rings. Platters of turkey were at the far end. Desserts were displayed on the sideboard in the dining room, while beverages were available from the bar in the conservatory. Everything was ready on time and looked and smelled delicious.

John removed his apron and hung it on a hook in the pantry. Maggie stepped in behind him and closed the door. He took her in his arms and pulled her close. "This is an odd moment to choose for some alone time." He planted a kiss on her neck.

She pushed him back. "Don't be silly. Susan and her family aren't here yet. They're never late—in fact, they usually arrive right after Sam and Joan to help set up." She let out an exasperated sigh. "I've called twice, and she doesn't answer."

"I'm sure there's a good explanation," John said. "Maybe Aaron got called into the hospital—or Julia's taking an extra-long nap."

"She would have called or texted me," Maggie said.

"Are you worried about them?"

"Not really. I'm sure you're right—there's a reason. The food is laid out and getting cold. We've got thirty-plus hungry people out there, waiting to eat. I came in here to ask if we should start without them?"

John opened his mouth to answer when the dogs erupted

again. "That'll be them," John said. "Shall we get out of this pantry before our guests begin to talk?"

Maggie laughed, and they stepped into the kitchen. David Wheeler and his mother Jackie had entered the room, with David's constant companion—therapy dog Dodger—at his side.

Glenn Vaughn crossed the kitchen in two long strides to greet the boy who he loved like a grandson. "I didn't know you were home for Thanksgiving," he said, pulling David into a tight hug.

Sam walked up behind them. "You're a sight for sore eyes," Sam said.

Glenn released David and made way for Sam and David to embrace. "I've missed you," Sam said. "My handyman business is a lonely affair without you as my second." Sam stepped back and held David at arm's length. "You look great. Learning to become a guide dog trainer agrees with you."

"I'm loving every minute of my time at the Guide Dog Center," David replied.

Gloria Vaughn joined her husband, Glenn. "We'll want to hear every detail," she said. "Please stop by our house for a visit while you're home. I'll make chocolate chip cookies for you to take back with you. How long will you be here?"

"We fly back on Sunday night," David said. "I have to work on Monday. I didn't get the long weekend off until yesterday. Mom got me on a standby flight this morning. That's why I didn't tell anyone I was coming home."

"We're happy you're here." Maggie hugged David and then Jackie.

"I'm sorry we came uninvited," Jackie said. "Since David wasn't supposed to be home for Thanksgiving, I didn't bother to buy food. After I booked his flight, I went to the grocery but only found one package of poultry—chicken wings. I told David we'd do pizza and wings this year, but he insisted we come to Rosemont. I hate to be a Thanksgiving crasher."

"You're no such thing," Maggie assured her. "You have a standing invitation. I'm sorry to think you would have stayed home alone if David hadn't come to town."

Jackie shrugged. "I'm never sure if people think I knew about William's embezzlement from the town. I feel you believe me, Maggie, but ..." she trailed off as she looked at the people scattered around the room. "Maybe some of them would rather not be near me."

Maggie leaned in so her words were heard by Jackie and no one else. "I know you had nothing to do with the mess William got himself into. Believe me, I understand what it feels like to be the wife of someone who committed and concealed crimes—and then died before you could ever understand what happened." She leaned back and looked into Jackie's eyes. "I'm positive that every person here feels the same way I do. You are among friends; you are welcome."

Jackie's lower lids brimmed with tears. She nodded and swiped her hands under her eyes.

Maggie's phone pinged in her pocket, alerting her to an

incoming text. She stepped away and opened the text from Susan.

> Got delayed. So very sorry. On our way soon. Please start without us.

Maggie searched the sea of faces for John and found him coming into the kitchen from the porch with David.

Four doggie faces now smeared wet noses against the glass as Dodger joined Roman, Eve, and Chance.

She caught John's eye and made a motion of bringing a fork to her lips.

John nodded his understanding. He grabbed a glass and struck it with a knife to silence the hubbub of conversation. "Thank you for being here today. Our Thanksgiving potluck is a tradition we cherish. The chance to spend the day with people we love so dearly means the world to Maggie and me. I want to introduce my new vet, Sherry Parker, and her husband, Neil" —he pointed to them— "and our friends from Linden Falls, Pam Olson and Steve Turner, who are standing next to Neil. If you haven't met them yet, please say hello."

"This is the most welcoming group I've ever encountered," Steve called out.

"I'm glad to hear that," John said. "And not surprised. Now—Sam will lead us in prayer, then everyone can go through the line and help themselves."

"There's plenty of food, so don't hold back," Maggie interjected. "Our goal is to consume a week's worth of calories in one sitting."

A titter of laughter ran through the crowd.

"Seat yourself at any of the tables and enjoy yourselves. We'll step outside at 5:30 for the lighting of the Christmas lights, then come back in to play games and sing carols. Our own Marc Benson will be at the piano again this year." He gestured to Marc, who stood with his partner Alex.

Marc took a bow.

"Dessert will be served as long as there's a piece of pie that hasn't been eaten. And now," —he turned to Sam— "let us give thanks for our many blessings."

Everyone lowered their heads as Sam voiced their shared gratitude. A chorus of "Amen" circled the room, and the meal was underway.

CHAPTER 38

Sherry leaned across the dinner table toward David. "I'm glad I've had the chance to get to know you. Frank Haynes raves about you every time he's at Westbury Animal Hospital with one of his dogs. He's over the moon about starting Forever Guides next door to Forever Friends."

"I'd hoped he and Loretta and the kids would be here tonight," David said. "He's the reason I'm at the Guide Dog Center."

"They decided to have a quiet day at home," Neil said. "Frank wanted to spend time with his family."

"How's he doing with that?" David asked. "Now that you're running Haynes Enterprises for him, is he home for dinner every night?"

Neil drew a deep breath and narrowed his eyes. "I think

Frank is one of those people who can't find the internal off switch."

"What do you mean?" David asked.

"He's working as hard as ever, but now it's on Forever Friends and the construction of Forever Guides."

"That's not good," David said. "I never wanted the guide dog school to keep him away from his family." He turned to Glenn on his right. "Are you and Tim Knudsen still having lunch with Frank once a week? How does he seem to you?"

Glenn speared a bite of his slice of apple pie with his fork. "We did our lunches for quite a while. He's canceled the last two weeks because he's been so busy. He told Tim that he's getting home in time for dinner but that he'll have to skip lunches for a while." Glenn looked at Neil. "From what you said, I take it he's not leaving on time."

"Let's put it this way—I'm out the door by six every night and Frank's still there."

"Sounds like it's time for Tim and me to talk to him again." He polished off his pie.

"I'll go see him," David said. "Tomorrow. He promised me he wouldn't work himself to death and I'm going to hold him to it."

Glenn looked at the young man. Coming to terms with his father's suicide had made him wise beyond his years. "I know he'd love to see you, son."

"That's brave of you," Neil said. "Don't get me wrong—he's terrific to work for—but I don't think he's open to advice."

"That's an understatement," Glenn said.

"I'll convince him he needs to hire someone to run Forever Friends," David said. "He loves it, just like he does Haynes Enterprises, but it's too much. If he's pouring his heart and soul into Forever Guides, he needs to find someone to help him with Forever Friends. It's worked out great with Haynes Enterprises" —he nodded toward Neil— "so it'll work for Forever Friends, too."

Glenn clapped David on the back. "I think you're right. Swing by our house tomorrow when you're done and fill me in on your progress. Tim and I will back you up when you return to California."

"Dodger and I will be there." He downed the piece of pumpkin pie on his plate in four bites.

"There's more pumpkin over there." Sherry gestured toward the sideboard. "Surely you've got room for more than one piece of pie."

David turned in his seat and considered the selection. "I can't decide between the chocolate cream and the pecan."

"You're young," Glenn said. "You can still eat like you have a hollow leg. Enjoy it while it lasts." He patted his rounded stomach. "Take one of each."

~

MAGGIE GLANCED down the length of her dining table. David was huddled in conversation with Glenn and the Parkers. By the expressions on their faces and the tautness in their shoulders, they were discussing something serious.

Gloria was seated next to Joan Torres, who was picking

with her fork at the bottom crust of the buttermilk pie she'd brought. Joan was shaking her head in consternation, while Gloria appeared to be reassuring her that the crust was as good as ever.

John sat to her right. He and Sam were critiquing, in intimate detail, the college football season and prognosticating about which team would be this year's champion.

Maggie sent up a prayer of thanks, as she often did, that she'd followed her instincts all those years ago and moved into Rosemont. She'd known no one here at the time, but now the love of her life was next to her and her home was filled with people she adored and who loved her back.

She was contemplating whether she had room for a tiny piece of Joan's buttermilk pie—so she could knowledgeably reassure her dear friend about the crust—when the dogs began to bark.

Maggie left her seat and walked toward the porch to check on them when Susan, Aaron, and Julia entered the kitchen.

"There you are! These guys announced your arrival," Maggie said.

"I'm so sorry we're late." Susan hugged her mother. "Happy Thanksgiving."

Julia spotted John in the dining room and made a beeline for the grandfather whom she had wrapped around her little finger.

"The same to you. Everything all right?" She looked at her daughter and was surprised to see that both she and her husband were blushing.

"Fine," Susan said. She turned to Aaron. "I left our pie in the car. Would you go get it?"

Aaron nodded and headed back the way he'd come in.

Susan took a deep breath. "We're trying again."

Maggie arched a brow.

"To get pregnant. It hasn't been as easy as the last time, so we've been tracking my ovulation."

Maggie tilted her head to one side, a smile touching her lips.

"Turns out *right now* was an ideal time. And Julia was still napping. So…"

Maggie pulled her daughter into a tight hug. "That's wonderful news. And the best reason to be late for Thanksgiving—*ever*."

"You're not mad?"

"Of course not."

"That's why I've been testy lately. Every time I get my period, I go into a complete funk."

"I'm sure this is very difficult," Maggie said.

"We'll talk more later," Susan said as Aaron rejoined them with the pie. "Right now, I want to take a slice of this pie to Sam—I know it's his favorite and I don't want him to miss out. Then we need to eat. I'm starved."

Maggie chuckled. "Sam was cruising the sideboard, searching for your pie. He looked crestfallen when it wasn't there. I told him you were running late and assured him you were still bringing your famous crustless cranberry pie."

Susan grinned. "It's nice to be known for something. Having people in Westbury associate a certain pie with me makes me feel like I belong here. It's a very Westburian kind of thing, no?"

"Yes. I agree completely."

Susan removed a slice of her pie, put it on a plate, and headed toward Sam.

"How's my favorite mother-in-law doing?" Aaron leaned down and kissed her cheek.

Maggie gestured around herself. "Life doesn't get better than this."

He nodded.

"There's plenty of everything. Fix yourself a plate. Your brother and Marc are in the conservatory, as usual."

"I'll get something for Julia first."

Maggie looked at the little girl, who was bouncing on John's knee as he made whinnying sounds. "John and I will make sure she gets fed. Right now, I don't think you could separate those two if you tried."

"You're right." Aaron picked up two plates and handed one to Susan as she joined him.

The doorbell rang, and the dogs erupted again.

"We're not the last ones, after all?" Susan asked her mother.

"That must be Sunday and Josh. They cooked their first Thanksgiving together for Robert and Lyla and promised to stop by here afterward for the evening festivities."

"Ooh," Susan remarked. "Sounds like they're getting serious if they're doing that."

"I hope so," Maggie said as she headed toward the door. "They're perfect for each other."

CHAPTER 39

Alistair:

I flitted upstairs for a rest after everyone arrived. Food no longer appealed to me, so watching people eat was boring. I'd reserve my energy for the after-dinner festivities I knew were sure to come. A rousing round of carol singing was one of my favorite things.

I'd also loosened one of the strings in the lower register of the piano. Marc would find it, of course. He always did. It was fun to see how long it took him to realize something was off and fix it. He was getting faster every year.

I had reached the living room when Maggie opened the door to two humans and two dogs.

Dan and Cara pranced at Josh and Sunday's feet, their noses lifted to sniff the delicious aromas wafting out to them.

"I hope this is okay," Sunday said, pointing to the dogs.

"Josh talked to John this morning when he called to let you know Robert and Lyla wouldn't be coming. Robert's still jet-lagged from his flight home from London." She took a breath and continued. "Anyway, John insisted we bring these two." She looked from the dogs to Josh, then back to Maggie. "I said I thought it was a bit much..."

I agreed with this intelligent young woman. Who brought their dogs with them when invited to dine?

"It's fine," Maggie said, stooping to scratch one set of ears and then the other. "One advantage of being married to a veterinarian is that pets are always welcome."

"Really?" If eyebrows could express doubt, Sunday's did just that.

"Absolutely. Step inside, out of the cold. We've got a special dog room, as a matter of fact. Roman and Eve are there, plus David's Dodger—you know Dodger?"

"Everyone knows Dodger," Josh said.

"Plus another enormous black Lab named Chance." Maggie patted Dan's head again. "You'll find someone who's the spitting image of you." She ushered them through the house to the porch, where Dan and Cara were enthusiastically welcomed by the other dogs. "Chance belongs to our new friends from Linden Falls. They're a young couple, here on their honeymoon."

"I'd like to meet them," Josh said.

"Follow me. The last time I looked, they were sitting in the library with Anita and Gordon, and Judy Young and Jeff Carson. I'll make the introductions."

We approached the table where Judy and Jeff were

pleading with Pam and Steve while Gordon and Anita looked on, amused.

"Maggie," Judy called to her friend as she entered the library with Josh and Sunday in tow. "Help us convince them."

"Of what?" Maggie smiled at everyone seated at the drop-leaf table. "First, let me introduce Sunday and Josh to Pam and Steve."

With pleasantries exchanged, Judy continued. "Pam and Steve should bring their home improvement TV show to Westbury."

"Haven't you finished renovating the Olsson House?"

"Yes. Jeff's just completed it. But the square is full of gorgeous historic homes that'll be demolished for something hideous if we don't restore them." She looked at the man she'd recently met and married—all because of her commitment to preserve the town's architectural history and a box of vintage ornaments stored in an attic. "Tell them, honey." She turned to her husband.

"I was saying how much I admire the show and the work that Duncan's Hardware has done to preserve the charm of Linden Falls. I wish I'd thought of that when I owned my hardware store. My son took it over when I retired and moved here. He's a big fan, too."

"Sam and Jeff have been talking about restoring another house on the square," Judy interjected. "I think your audience would love to follow along."

Anita joined in. "I agree."

Maggie smiled at the newlyweds. "It seems like we're

ganging up on you, but I think they're right. A project like that could take you to the next level."

"I've got an idea," Gordon said. "Perhaps Judy and Jeff could give you a tour of the Olsson House they've recently renovated? Discuss a new project after you see what they've done. If you have time before you leave."

"We're heading back in the morning," Pam said ruefully. She glanced at Steve. "We've driven through the residential area by the square. It's gorgeous, and we noted several homes with terrific curb appeal already."

"Come by the house for breakfast on your way out of town," Judy said. "I open Celebrations at ten, so stop by as early as you'd like."

Steve looked at Pam, who nodded almost imperceptibly. "You people here in Westbury are extremely persuasive."

Judy clasped her hands. "It's settled. See you at eight."

"I love it," Maggie said. "A TV deal may have been struck right here in Rosemont's library."

Political careers have been launched and fortunes made and lost in this library, I thought.

"That's not all," Pam said. "Anita and Gordon told us about Anita's plans to open a sewing machine museum in Westbury. My mother loves to sew. I asked them to keep me posted. My mom and I will be the first visitors at the grand opening."

"Hold on," Anita said. "I don't have an existing show like you do. My museum is still a dream. I've got to find a location, file paperwork, obtain permits—and I don't know if anyone other than Pam and her mother will be interested."

"I can help with that," Sunday said.

All eyes turned to her.

"The Highpointe Library has a lot of unused space, now that we've digitized our records. Josh and Lyla and I discussed over our Thanksgiving dinner using that space for traveling exhibits that will bring people into the library."

"That's a fabulous plan!" Maggie said. "Nice work, Sunday."

"I can't take credit for it—it was Josh's idea." She flashed her thousand-watt smile at him.

"The exhibits should appeal to students *and* the wider community," he supplied. "They don't need to be book related. I'll bet the local watercolors club—or marble aficionados—or someone who collects yoyos would be thrilled to put up an exhibit. We could change them out quarterly. That would keep people coming back who might not go to a library otherwise."

"The inaugural exhibit could be vintage sewing machines. We'll house it in a separate room at the front and keep track of how many people view it. That'll give you an idea of how popular your museum might be."

"Could she post something that announces a museum will be coming soon?" Gordon asked.

"Yes. Brilliant." Sunday's eyes shone. "This would be a wonderful way to start our new exhibition series. Please say yes."

Anita looked at Gordon, who nodded. "It sounds perfect. When can I see your space?"

"I'm off tomorrow, but I'd love to take you through it

then. The library will be almost deserted since so many students go home for Thanksgiving. I don't know how much time it will take you to get your sewing machines ready, but I'd love to open the exhibit in early January."

"Then we'd better get cracking. Shall we say nine?" Gordon asked. "That is, if you'd like me to go with you, Anita?"

"You know I would," she replied.

"Wow," Maggie said. "This is the power table, for sure. Look at what you've come up with!"

The sky outside the library windows had grown progressively darker as they talked. Guests from the other rooms were heading to the front door. It was almost time for the outside lights to come on. I loved this Christmas tradition even more than carol singing. These people in the library needed to stop talking and get out there.

I zoomed into the foyer and allowed the front door to slip out of Alex's hand, banging open against the door frame. A blast of cold air hit the group at the table in the library and caused them to turn their attention to the archway into the foyer.

"It's time for lights!"

"We don't want to miss those," Anita cried, leaping to her feet. "Gordon and John worked so hard to put them up."

Everyone in the library followed the rest of the guests down the stone steps to take their positions on the driveway.

John found Gordon in the crowd and sidled up next to him. "Here we go. It'll be any moment now."

Gordon glanced at his watch and nodded.

The front facade of Rosemont sprung into illumination, and its intricate roofline and eaves hung with icicle lights. Every shrub was covered in white fairy lights and the trunks of the trees were wound with them. Thousands of tiny white lights twinkled against the night sky.

I joined the assembled crowd in drawing a collective breath. The invitees erupted in cheers and applause without me.

John turned to Gordon and extended his hand. The men shared a satisfied handshake.

Maggie came up behind them. "Congratulations, you two. Rosemont is more spectacular than ever."

John slipped his hand around her waist. The three of them hung back as the guests returned to the house. A jazzy rendition of "Hark! The Herald Angels Sing" floated out to them through the open door.

We paused for one more look at the beauty of Rosemont, then joined the party inside.

CHAPTER 40

David drove by the street entrance to Forever Friends.

Dodger, sitting alert in the shotgun seat, let out an excited bark. He placed his paws on the armrest and turned his attention to the window, which he decorated with wet nose prints.

"Excited to be back here, boy?" David asked the dog Glenn and Frank had arranged for him to receive from Forever Friends—the dog who had turned his life around. "Me, too. We'll go in the back way to say hi to everybody."

He turned at the edge of the building and followed the road around to the employee parking lot. Even though he wasn't working there while he attended guide dog training school, the employee entrance felt natural to him.

David raised both eyebrows when he saw Frank's car parked in its usual spot. He and Dodger had come from

Frank and Loretta's home, where he'd gone looking for Frank. Loretta had told him that Frank and Sean were shopping for the family Christmas tree. She'd invited him to come back to help them decorate the tree and said she'd text David when Frank and Sean got home.

David had agreed. He would have found a way to pull Frank aside to talk to him. But now that Frank was at Forever Friends, having a private conversation with his mentor and father-figure would be easier.

He parked next to Frank's car, and he and Dodger went inside. They were warmly welcomed by volunteers and staff members, who bombarded him with questions about his experiences at the Guide Dog Center. Dodger was showered with pets, rubs, and treats.

Sean caught sight of them at the end of the hall. "David," the middle-schooler cried as he ran up to them.

"How're you doing, man?" David asked. The two fist-bumped. "It looks like you're having a busy day, considering all the commotion."

Sean nodded. "We've reduced adoption fees for the weekend," he said. "Since everyone else has Black Friday sales, we thought we'd try it."

"Great idea." David looked at the boy he'd worked with during the summer before leaving for school. He knew Sean wanted to step into David's shoes when he was gone. "It looks like you're doing a wonderful job. The place looks terrific."

Sean shrugged, but his cheeks flushed under the praise. "You taught me well."

"How much time do you spend here?"

"I come every day after school. I take the bus, and Frank and I are supposed to come home for dinner by six."

"Supposed to?"

"We used to leave on time, but Frank's been working late ever since we've received the architect's plans for Forever Guides. He says he's dealing with contractor bids, zoning issues, permits, and financing."

"I'm sure it's a lot," David said. "So, what time do you get home?"

"I take the bus and am home for dinner. Mom insists. Frank …" his voice trailed off. "Frank gets home later and later. Last week he wasn't even there before my sisters and I went to bed." He turned sad eyes to David.

David pursed his lips. It seemed his workaholic friend was at it again. "I just left your house, and your mom told me you and Frank were getting your Christmas tree."

"Frank said he needed to stop by here—real quick, he said—and then we'd go to the tree lot." Sean rolled his eyes. "He's been telling me 'ten more minutes' for the past hour and a half."

"Is he in his office?"

Sean nodded.

"We'll go say hi."

Sean turned to go with them.

"Would you mind taking Dodger to the exercise yard while I talk to Frank? He loved it out there. I'm sure he'd rather run around outside."

Sean squared his shoulders. "Sure. You can trust Dodger with me."

David handed him the dog's leash. "I know he's in good hands with you." He watched as Sean and Dodger, his tail held high and wagging like a metronome set at prestissimo, exited the building.

⁓

"Ten more minutes, son. I mean it this time." Frank uttered the words without looking up as he hunched over the architectural plans spread out on his desk.

"Hey, Frank," David said from the open doorway.

Frank spun around in his chair. "David!" He ripped the reading glasses off his face and tossed them on his desk as he sprang to his feet. "You didn't tell me you were coming home for Thanksgiving." He crossed the room in two strides to greet the boy who had become like a son to him.

"Mom got me a ticket home at the last minute. I decided I'd surprise you."

Frank released David and looked into his eyes. "You're happy—and content. This program suits you, doesn't it?"

"I'm learning so much. You wouldn't believe it. I thought I knew a lot about dogs before I went, but now?" David shook his head slowly.

"I want to hear everything," Frank said, pointing to a chair next to his desk.

"Aren't you and Sean supposed to be picking out the

Christmas tree?" He recounted his conversation with Loretta.

Frank bit his lip. "You're right. Sean and I need to get going. As soon as I finish..." His eyes drifted to his paper-strewn desk.

"I'll fill you in on my time in California when I come over to help decorate the tree," David said. "Right now, I want to talk to you about how you're doing, Frank."

"I'm fine," Frank said. "Neil Parker's taken over the operation of Haynes Enterprises and he's doing a fabulous job. I hate to admit it, but he's brought a fresh perspective to the business and implemented terrific improvements. He's a better chief operating officer than I ever was."

"I'm glad to hear that."

"I'm grateful to you that you made me see I needed to make changes. I followed through, and it's worked out."

"Good." David drew a deep breath. "Because I think you need to make more changes."

Frank shifted in his chair. "What do you mean?"

"I've heard that you're working late again—"

"Once or twice," Frank interrupted. "Launching a new business—setting it up for success—takes time."

"I've been told—by multiple sources—that it's every night now." Frank opened his mouth to protest, and David held up a hand to silence him. "Look at what you're doing right now: you've been working in your office for the past two hours when you're supposed to be buying a Christmas tree. Your family is home, waiting for you, Frank."

Frank turned his face aside.

"It's the same old story. Like right after the twins were born. I was afraid we'd lose you to a heart attack or something worse." David's face grew pale. "Suicide. Like my dad." He paused, collecting himself. "You're a workaholic—it's your default setting."

Frank inhaled deeply and exhaled slowly. "I keep telling myself, if I just finish one more task, things will settle down. I'm the most qualified person to manage the formation of our new guide dog school. Starting businesses is what I do best."

"Then hire someone to run Forever Friends for you—like you did with Haynes Enterprises. You can still handle Forever Guides, but you can't do both of them."

Frank leaned forward in his chair and stared at David.

"Is it the money? Can you afford to pay someone else to do the work?"

"That's not a problem. Haynes Enterprises is doing better than ever."

"Maybe the new manager of Forever Friends will make improvements you haven't thought of—like Neil Parker has." David held his breath, waiting for Frank's response.

Frank nodded his head with increasing conviction. "You're right," he said. "I don't know why I didn't think of it. I guess it's a forest and trees thing."

David's posture relaxed. "I'm so relieved you've agreed. It may take some time to find the right person, but you'll find them."

Frank lifted his chin, and his eyes gleamed. "I already

know who'd be perfect for the job. They could start at Forever Friends and work with me at Forever Guides, too."

"Wow. Do I know this person?"

"I don't think so. I'll make an offer next week."

"Are you going to keep this person's identity a secret?"

"For now. Let's see if they accept first." He grinned at David. "Do you want to come with Sean and me to get our tree?"

"Sure. My mom is shopping with her sister. We're going to dinner and a movie tonight, so I'm free until four."

"Then let's get going." Frank turned out his desk lamp and grabbed his jacket from the back of his chair.

They headed down the hallway side-by-side. Frank put his arm across David's shoulders. "Thanks for watching out for me, son."

CHAPTER 41

Maggie unlocked her office an hour earlier than usual. She loved being the first one in —especially first thing on a Monday. Gordon had left the morning before for the long trip home. After the hubbub of the weekend, she'd spent the rest of Sunday running laundry, cleaning out the fridge, and straightening up the house. She was hoping, now, to put things in order in her office before the busy week began.

She hung her coat, stashed her purse, and made a pot of coffee before she settled in front of her computer. She was making quick progress through her inbox when one message —time stamped at 2:04 a.m.—caught her eye.

She opened the email from Yolanda Yates that had come through without a subject line. She read the sentence once, then reread it.

You'll see my response. Have a nice day.

What in the world? Maggie knew Yolanda was taunting her. She picked up her phone and tapped her social media app. Yolanda had tagged her in the post.

Paul Martin had a second family. Do we really think he wasn't sexually harassing women? And Maggie Martin knew about it. My husband has been accused of crimes Paul Martin committed. Why has she kept silent—is it because she wants my husband's job? Tell me what you think in the comments. #sexualharrassment #MeToo #MaggieMartin #backstabbingbitch

Maggie recoiled against the back of her chair so hard she knocked her coffee cup over, sending a wave of steaming liquid racing to the edge of her desk. She lunged for the tissue box on her credenza and tore out handfuls of tissues that she threw onto the mess. After corralling most of the liquid, she went to the reception area to get a roll of paper towels from the cabinet beneath the coffee maker.

Josh entered the reception area as she was returning the unused towels and discarding a large wad of coffee-soaked tissues and towels.

"I thought you weren't coming in until after your exam," she said.

"I wasn't, but …" he hesitated, eyeing her closely. "You don't look so good."

"I spilled a full cup of coffee across my desk. I got some of it on my slacks while I was cleaning it up." She rolled her eyes. "It'll dry. I'll run home at lunch to change."

"That's all?"

It was Maggie's turn to scrutinize him. "You've seen it, haven't you?"

Josh nodded. "That woman is pure poison."

"That was my initial reaction." Maggie sighed. "But deep down, I think she's scared to death. She's clinging to a reality that doesn't exist—that her husband is the good man she thought she married and none of what he's been accused of is true. I feel sorry for her."

Josh's expression remained stern.

"You think I'm taking this too lightly?"

"I do. You can't let this stand. Call the PR team and the lawyers. You're extremely capable at a tremendous variety of things but handling a social media smear campaign isn't one of them. It's time to take your daughter's advice."

Maggie buttoned her jacket and smoothed her hair. "You're right. I've tried to manage Yolanda on my own—and failed miserably. I'll call Susan."

Josh's shoulders relaxed. "You'll call right now?"

"I promise."

"And you'll follow her advice?"

"Yes!" Maggie's voice was steely in its resolve. "If you came in this morning to make sure I handle the situation, you don't need to worry. Go back home—or to the library—to study until your test."

Josh set his backpack on his desk. "I'll go over my notes here, if that's okay. I'll screen your calls and handle anything from the trustees."

Maggie put her hand to her forehead. "The trustees—I forgot about them. Do you think I'll hear from them?"

Josh nodded. "Based on Yolanda's statement that you're

trying to get her husband's job, yes, they'll want to hear from you."

Maggie headed for her office. "It's ridiculous! My husband's veterinary practice is in Westbury, we both love Rosemont, and I've never been happier in a job than as President of Highpointe. I'll prepare a denial to send to the trustees as soon as I've talked to Susan."

Maggie was about to place the call when her cell phone buzzed with an incoming call from her daughter.

"You've seen it, I assume," Susan said without exchanging greetings.

"Yes."

"Have you done anything?"

"No. I had planned to call you first, then I'll reach out to the PR team and lawyers. After that, I'm going to email the chairman of the board of trustees to assure him I'm *not* looking for a new job—whether Malcolm Yates' job or anywhere else."

"Good. Draft that email but hold off on contacting the PR team or lawyers. I've got an idea."

"What are you planning?"

"I'd rather not say until I've worked on it a bit."

"Oh ... okay."

"Do you trust me, Mom?"

"Of course I do!"

"Then sit tight. Don't worry. And stop looking at that stupid post! It'll only upset you more."

"You're right about *that*."

"I'll call when I've got something," Susan said and the line went dead.

Maggie shut her eyes and inhaled and exhaled five big breaths. The calming technique didn't have much effect, so she repeated it two more times. Feeling a tiny bit better, she pulled up her email and began crafting her message to the trustees.

CHAPTER 42

Susan pulled into the driveway of Frank and Loretta's home just before nine. She'd texted Loretta early that morning. Loretta had told her the kids would be in school, the twins would be down for their morning naps, and she'd have time to meet with Susan then.

The front door opened as Susan approached the door. Loretta motioned her inside. "I didn't want the doorbell to wake Branson and Bonnie," she said in a muted voice. "Especially since Ingrid's on vacation until tomorrow."

Susan nodded and tiptoed into the family room after Loretta.

Loretta closed the double doors behind them and pointed to the baby monitor on the mantel below the television. The sounds of rhythmic baby breathing provided background noise. Sally and Snowball lay on their dog beds, also fast asleep. Daisy opened one eye and raised her head to scrutinize Susan. Satisfied that the visitor posed no threat, she lowered it to her paws and went back to sleep.

"I'm sorry to barge in on you, Loretta." Susan lowered herself to the sofa.

"I already know why you're here." Loretta paced in front of her.

"You saw Yolanda's post?"

Loretta nodded. "And I know what I need to do."

Susan waited for her to continue.

"I'm going to come forward—as the other woman. I'll say that Paul never harassed me and I'm certain he never did that to anyone else. Maggie knew nothing about me or my kids, but she—and the entire family—has been kind, gracious, and loving to us since she met us." Loretta knelt in front of Susan and grasped her hands. "And I'll tell everyone that you donated a kidney to save Nicole's life." She choked on the next words. "The half-sister you never knew you had."

Susan leaned into Loretta and hugged her. "Thank you," she whispered.

Loretta nodded and pulled back to face Susan. "Is that why you wanted to see me?"

"Yes. I was going to ask you to do what you've just described."

"Do you think it will help Maggie? She doesn't deserve this hateful nonsense." Loretta cleared her throat. "And neither does your father. He did some bad, dishonorable things, but he wasn't a sexual predator."

"I'm glad to hear you say that," Susan said.

"I'm sure this has been terrible for you, too," Loretta said.

"It has," Susan admitted. "I want Yolanda to stop bringing my parents into her problem."

"Would you like to see what I've written?" Loretta stood and pulled her laptop from the coffee table. She handed it to Susan. "I prepared it but haven't posted yet."

Susan's eyes traveled across the screen. "It's perfect. Don't change a word."

"Thanks," Loretta replied.

"Does Frank know about this?"

"He does."

"And he's on board with your response? It'll bring unwanted attention to your family."

Loretta paused, searching for the right words. "He realizes that my relationship with Paul became common knowledge in Westbury years ago when you donated your kidney to Nicole. He appreciates Maggie's support following his fraud convictions and now wants to assist her, but he has concerns about the children. They're older now—their friends are older, too. Frank thinks we need to talk to them before we send this out. They need to learn what's going on from us before they hear it at school, from other kids." The lines around Loretta's eyes deepened as she looked at Susan. "Would it be all right with you and Maggie if we wait to send this out until we talk to the big kids after school?"

Susan nodded. "That makes perfect sense. We don't want them to be blindsided."

Loretta's face relaxed. "That's the plan. Frank promised he will pick up the kids when school gets out and we'll talk to them as soon as they get home. I'll post this immediately"

—she pointed to the laptop screen again— "and text you to let you know it's done."

"Thank you, Loretta." Susan stood and the two women hugged.

"You were there for me and my child when we needed it. You can always count on me to be there for you."

CHAPTER 43

Frank greeted Josh in the reception area of Forever Friends. "Thank you for stopping by on such short notice," Frank said.

"Sure," Josh said. "I just completed my last exam for the semester and Maggie gave me the rest of the day off."

"Let's talk in my office." Frank led the way. "You enjoy working for Maggie?"

"She's great, and I've learned a ton from her, but I'll graduate this spring and need to move on."

Frank motioned for Josh to take the seat opposite his desk. "I should have asked—would you like coffee? Water?"

"Thank you, but I'm good," Josh said.

"Are you looking for a new job?"

"Yes."

"How's it going?"

"The search itself is a full-time job." Josh's shoulders

drooped. "I've been applying across the region, including at Highpointe. I'd like to settle in Westbury."

"Have you found anything that suits you?"

"I've got an offer that would be a good stepping stone to other positions I'd be more interested in." He shrugged. "The pay is good, but it's three hours away. I'd like to find something closer to Westbury, but time's running out. They want an answer from me next week. If I don't have another offer before then, I'm going to take it."

Frank rested his elbows on his desktop and leaned toward Josh. "I know you've worked hard to get your master's degree and understand that you'd want to find a job using it."

"That's the idea." Josh gave Frank a half smile.

"Would you be interested in an opportunity that might not use your degree right away—but could, eventually?"

"What do you mean?"

"I've been terribly impressed by your Doggie Day Out program. It's barely started, and it's already been wildly successful. Every dog chosen for a day out has been adopted and the publicity has brought people into the shelter who adopt other animals."

"I'm pleased with the community response."

"You're a young man with ideas and the ability to carry them out. You also have a heart for rescues and strays. That's as important as good ideas and implementation skills. This job requires heart."

Josh sat up straighter in his chair.

Frank waved his hands across the architectural plans and

documents spread across his desk. "I'm up to my eyeballs in projects relating to Forever Guides. Drowning in work, to be truthful."

"It's a huge project," Josh agreed.

"A close friend—the young man who started me on this path—was home from school this past weekend and reminded me I need help."

"Is that David Wheeler?"

"You know him?"

"I met him at Rosemont on Thanksgiving. *The Westbury Gazette* has written about him and Dodger, too. He's a remarkable young man."

"He is," Frank replied. "He convinced me to hire someone to run Forever Friends for me so I can concentrate on getting Forever Guides built and operational. I'd like to offer that position to you."

Josh stared at him. "I've never run a business," he stammered.

"You'd figure it out in a flash," Frank said. "There's a vacant office next to this one. I'll be here if you have questions. What makes you the ideal candidate is that your degree qualifies you to run an educational institution." Frank's words came faster as he continued. "Forever Guides will be a school to teach people how to train guide dogs. Students will come from across the country, and even the world. We'll need curriculum, tuition, housing, certifications, and more. I don't know a thing about any of that, but you do." He looked at Josh.

"I could handle that."

"You'd get in on the ground floor of an organization with a life-changing mission. The position would give you the chance to use everything you've learned while getting your degree." Frank dropped his hands to his desk. "Are you interested?"

"Yes—I sure am." A smile sliced across Josh's face.

"Good. You'll have full benefits and a retirement plan. I don't know how much this sort of position pays because I've always run Forever Friends myself." Frank narrowed his eyes in thought. "Since you're happy with the amount you'd make at this other job you've been offered, I'll pay you the same as that. Is that attractive?"

Josh's smile super-sized itself. "That would be wonderful!"

The timer on Frank's phone sounded. "I've got to leave to pick up the kids from school. I can't be late." He stood. "You'll accept the position—Director of Forever Friends?"

"Yes. Thank you!"

Frank and Josh shook hands. "Welcome aboard. When can you start?"

"Can I work part-time until I graduate?"

"Sure. I assume you'll want to give Maggie plenty of notice and train your replacement?"

"I will."

"I've got to go. Let's talk again next week." Frank stepped out of his office, with Josh at his heels. He pointed to the closed door next to his. "That'll be your office," he said. "Take a look at it now, if you want." He began striding toward the employee entrance. "Let me know if you need anything to make it functional for you," he called to Josh before exiting into the parking lot.

Josh stared down the long hallway. The kennels were to his right and the get-acquainted rooms to his left. The faint aroma of cleaning supplies melded with the stronger smells of dogs and cats. He would run this place!

A staff member ushered an older couple and a dachshund to one of the get-acquainted rooms.

Josh's heart flooded with happiness. Witnessing people adopt a pet was like watching them fall in love. Everyone was a kid again, experiencing the rush of infatuation that inevitably turned into a deep bond.

He turned back to what would become his office, opened the door, and flipped on the overhead light. A large window looked out on the exercise area. The desk and chair had seen better days and the aluminum blinds at the window were yellowed. It was a far cry from the elegant furnishings of the Office of the President of Highpointe College. He couldn't care less.

Josh's delight at being able to remain in Westbury—in an interesting job with a promising future—filled him with a joy that was palpable.

What had Sunday told him, when he'd been discouraged during his job search? That things would all work out. They certainly had.

Josh closed the door of his office and headed for the front door. He knew what he wanted to do next. He checked the time on his phone. If he didn't run into traffic, he'd make it to the bank before it closed.

CHAPTER 44

"Thanks for picking up the kids on time," Loretta murmured to Frank as he followed Marissa, Sean, and Nicole in from the garage.

"Sure," he said. "Let's talk to the kids and then go out to dinner."

"You're not going back to the office?"

He shook his head. "I'm home for the rest of the day. And I'll be home for dinner from now on, like I promised."

She raised her eyebrows in surprise and was about to speak when Marissa interrupted them.

"Frank said you have something to talk to us about." Her eyes telegraphed her fear. "What's up? Is one of you sick?"

Sean and Nicole lined up next to their older sister and looked at Loretta and Frank. All three of them were curious and unnerved about the upcoming talk.

"Nothing of the kind," Loretta reassured her. "We want

you to hear something from us, but it doesn't involve our family." She furrowed her brows. "Not our immediate family, that is—not the people who live in this house," she sputtered. "Let's go into the family room."

Bonnie and Branson were awake in their swings. They waved their arms and kicked their feet in greeting when they saw Frank and their siblings.

"You can play with the twins later," Frank said. "For now, take a seat on the sofa."

The kids complied, and Frank went to stand next to Loretta.

She cleared her throat and began. "There's a woman on social media who has been posting nasty, untrue things about Nicole and Susan's dad. She's been hateful toward Maggie, too." She looked from one child to the next. "Have any of you seen these posts?"

They each shook their head no.

"People trash talk others on social media all the time," Marissa said. "It's so mean. And it doesn't matter if it's true or not."

"Exactly," Loretta said. "These posts might hurt Maggie at her job."

"That sucks," Sean said. "They shouldn't get away with that."

"We agree," Frank said. "Your mother and I can help Maggie."

"I'm going to post about how Paul Martin is Nicole's biological father—and how kind Susan was to donate her kidney to Nicole. Maggie didn't know about Paul and me, and she's been kind and supportive of our family since she found out. I hope that will put an end to this woman's smear campaign on social media."

"Your mom's not asking your permission to do this. She's made up her mind and has her post ready to go. We want you to know what's going on so that if any of the kids at school ask you about it you won't be in the dark."

"Some of what I'm going to say is personal and private information. I hate the thought that kids might be nasty to you, but I feel morally bound to speak up for Maggie."

Marissa and Sean exchanged a glance, then Sean spoke. "Our family story is already old news at school. I doubt anyone will care."

"Even if they do, standing up for Maggie is the right thing to do. Maggie acts like a grandmother, and Susan is our big sister. Both of them treat us like genuine family."

Nicole hopped to her feet. "I love Susan and Maggie," she said, thrusting her fists down at her sides. "We can't let anyone bully them."

Loretta brought her hands to her heart. "I'm relieved to hear you feel this way. Not surprised, but relieved … and proud."

"If you get any sort of blowback about this, you're to let one of us know." Frank looked from one child to the next as they nodded their agreement.

"You're not to respond. No handling things on your own," Loretta added.

Again, the children nodded.

"I'm going to post it now," Loretta walked to her open laptop and pressed send. "Would you like to see the posts?"

"Maybe later," Sean said. "Dad said we could go to Tomascino's for pizza when we were done. I'm starved."

"I'll look at it after dinner," Marissa said. "I'm hungry, too."

"Let's wrestle these guys into car seats and hit the road," Loretta said. "I'm ready to celebrate a family dinner with pepperoni and extra cheese."

CHAPTER 45

Alistair:

Soft footsteps on the stairway at four in the morning drew my attention. I loved floating around downstairs, on my own, in the middle of the night. I usually straightened the pictures. Sometimes I transported keys from a spot where they'd been carelessly dropped to the location where they usually lived—where I knew my people would look for them in the morning. Sometimes I enjoyed seeing them race around—tearing up and down the stairs—frantically searching for their keys. This spectacle had proved less entertaining as I became increasingly attached to my people over the years.

I entered the living room in time to see Maggie hurrying down the stairs on her slippered feet, tying the sash of her furry robe as she went. The little dog was at her feet.

John sometimes got up this early. He often left the house

before five when he had surgeries to perform. I was proud that an esteemed doctor lived at Rosemont.

Maggie's job was important, too, but didn't require her to be out the door before dawn.

I watched as she entered the library and sat at the desk.

Blossom, Bubbles, and Buttercup were sound asleep in their favorite perches in the library. I sensed they knew she was in the room but were still mad about being boarded at Westbury Animal Hospital while Gordon was our house guest. They'd been happy to come home after Gordon left but would give Maggie and John the cold shoulder for a few more days. *Cats....*

Maggie opened her laptop. "We're going to check to see if Yolanda responded to Loretta's post," she said, "and then go right back to bed." She reached down and stroked the dog, who stared up at her with adoration. "You shouldn't have gotten up with me, Eve."

Eve pressed her muzzle into Maggie's hand.

"You know I've been upset by this, don't you, girl? I tossed and turned all night." Maggie slid her chair away from the desk and patted her lap.

Eve accepted the invitation and leapt into her owner's lap.

Maggie leaned over the dog and tapped on the keyboard.

The screen came to life.

Maggie moved the image on the screen up and down. She did this with increasing speed. Back and forth. She tapped on the keyboard and scrolled some more.

"Loretta's post is up and there are hundreds of

comments." She pursed her lips as she read them. "All but a couple of them are on Loretta's side. Yolanda's getting trashed. But I can't find Yolanda's anywhere." She looked at Eve, who raised her eyes to meet Maggie's.

"Let's see if there's anything on my personal email."

I moved myself into position behind her and stared at what she was fixated on.

"Here's an email from Susan. She says Yolanda's taken down her entire social media account." Maggie drew in a sharp breath. "Susan thinks that's a positive development. She says it's perfect timing. No one will be talking about me when I go to that conference next week."

Eve thumped her tail against Maggie's thigh.

"I'm not so sure, girl." She sank into the chair. "Yolanda lashed out in fear and anger. Going silent—running away—isn't the answer. I hope she's getting help. I've been in her shoes. You need someone in your corner to survive what she's going through." She scooped the dog off of her lap and held her close. "Like you. When you appeared—amid that snowstorm on my first morning at Rosemont—you saved me, girl."

I straightened my shoulders in pride. Finding the lost terrier mix in the ditch along the side of the road and guiding her up the long driveway to Rosemont had been my doing. She'd been wet and cold and scared, but had the good sense to trust me.

I knew the nice woman had fallen asleep in the big chair by the French doors into the library. Eve had followed my lead and settled herself on the other side of those French doors.

I'd made enough noise to rouse Maggie. When Eve had seen her moving, she'd joined in. Maggie had unlocked the door, ushered the sweet creature inside, and the rest, as they say, is history.

Maggie closed her laptop and deposited Eve on the rug. "I think we'd better go back to bed."

She headed toward the stairway, with Eve—and me—at her heels.

CHAPTER 46

Sunday read over her text response to Josh. He'd invited her over for dinner, saying he had news that couldn't wait.

Can't do dinner. Working until 8. Covering for the reference librarian who went home sick. Want me to stop by your place after I get off work?

She pursed her lips and tapped send. His message could only mean one thing—he'd gotten the financial aid job that he'd interviewed for. They'd joked that they could cope with being in a long-distance relationship, but the thought made her heart hurt. Josh had been by her side every day since that awful night in this very library, when Nigel Blythe had tried to kill her. She shuddered involuntarily.

His text pinged, and she smiled as she read his response.

YES!!! Let's walk along the fancy homes behind the square and look at their Christmas lights, too. You love that.

She hearted his message and opened a new browser on her computer. If he was moving, she wanted to go with him. Her position at the Highpointe Library was her dream job, but being close to him was more important. She'd search for a new dream job.

Sunday typed reference librarian jobs into the search bar, together with the name of the city. Her query produced one page of results. She picked up a pen and a pad of paper and began making notes as she scrolled through them.

Meanwhile, across town, Josh was making plans of his own.

He cast one last glance at the vintage diamond and sapphire engagement ring that had belonged to his mother and his paternal grandmother before her. If Sunday wanted something different, they'd sell this ring and get her what she wanted. Burman Jewelers had checked that the settings were secured. Harriet had told him it would easily sell for ten thousand dollars, but it would take time for the right buyer to come along.

He snapped the lid shut on the royal-blue, velvet ring box Harriet had insisted on giving him, free of charge. Sunday loved vintage items; his gut told him she'd love this ring.

Cara and Dan circled at his feet. "She can't come to dinner," he told them. "We're going for an after-dinner walk, which means we'll take the two of you." He dropped to one knee and took Cara's muzzle in his hand. "No running after squirrels," he admonished. "You guys will be witnesses. That's a huge responsibility. You have to be on your best behavior."

The dogs sat in front of him, wagging their tails with serious expressions on their faces, as if they understood.

"It'll be dark soon," he continued. "Let's scope out our route and find the perfect spot."

Again, the dogs wagged their agreement.

∼

Josh pulled his car into a space at the curb near the Olsson House.

"Would you look at that!" Sunday's voice was full of wonder as she leaned forward to peer out the windshield. "Don't tell Maggie I said this, but it's as beautifully decorated as Rosemont."

"She told me the same thing yesterday," Josh said. "And she's happy about it."

Sunday turned in her seat. "This entire street is lit up. I can't believe it isn't bumper to bumper with cars."

Josh bit his tongue. He almost told her it had been earlier, when he'd come to find "the spot."

"It probably gets busy closer to Christmas."

"I hope so," Sunday said. "The whole town needs to see this."

"Are you sure you don't mind walking a few blocks?"

"I'm not going to want to stop at a few blocks," Sunday said. "You can see everything so much better on foot. Besides, it's not too cold and there's no wind. The dogs will want a nice walk."

They got out of the car, and Josh released Dan and Cara

from their doggie car seats. He leaned into them and whispered, "remember—best behavior," before handing Cara's leash to Sunday.

He double-checked that the ring box was tied shut and firmly attached to Dan's collar.

The foursome set out.

They walked by a house where every surface was decked out in flashing, multicolored lights. Christmas carols blared from speakers mounted on the roof.

"There's a lot going on there," Sunday said. "I prefer something ... calmer."

Josh nodded, his mind rehearsing the words he'd prepared.

The Olsson House was next. White icicle lights traced the roofline and were wound through the ironwork gates. The tree trunks were closely wrapped with single-color strands of lights in red, green, blue, and gold.

"This is more my style," Sunday said.

Josh took her free hand in his and held it as they walked. There were two more houses on this street. Then they'd turn the corner and be there.

Sunday approved of the Disney-themed animatronics of the next house. "I was a Disney princess kid, and the only thing better than regular Disney princesses are ones in Christmas gowns."

The last house on the block was given over to a Star Wars theme. Sunday slid her eyes to Josh. "You like this, don't you?"

He shrugged and nodded.

"To each his own," she said.

They reached the end of the block. He led them to the right.

"I thought you had news that couldn't wait?"

"I do. Just a little further. I want the perfect backdrop."

"Okay …"

They rounded the corner and walked past a tall stand of trees. A small storybook cottage sat back from the curb. Stone steps led to an arched front door. Symmetrical, oblong windows fanned out on either side. The honey-colored stucco was decorated with ornate wooden carvings in a rich espresso color. Every detail was outlined in tiny white lights. Snow clung to the steep roof and glittered in the moonlight.

Sunday inhaled sharply and stopped in her tracks. "This looks like a gingerbread house," she said, bringing her hand to her throat. "Like a real-life one!"

"Do you like it?"

"Are you kidding me? It's the most charming house I've ever seen. This is my dream house. I can't believe I've never noticed it before."

Josh pointed to the trees lining the walkway to the steps, now bare except for twinkle lights. "I think we won't be able to see it in spring and summer—but we'll come back to find out."

Dan placed one of his front paws on Sunday's thigh.

"You like it, too, don't you, boy?" She leaned sideways to ruffle the fur on his neck. Her hand collided with a small box affixed to his collar. "What's this?"

Josh took her hands and brought them to his chest. "I've

watched YouTube videos of grand, romantic settings. I'm afraid this isn't in that category." He glanced at the house. "Still—I thought you'd love this place. You deserve something fancy, but this is the best I've got."

He dropped to one knee, keeping hold of her hands. He looked into her eyes and said the words they'd both longed he would say. "I adore you, Sunday Sloan. I want us to build a life together and share the journey for the rest of our lives. Will you marry me?"

Sunday dropped to her knees and gazed into his eyes. "Yes." She began to cry. "I love you, too. And I'm ready to move with you. We'll build a happy life together wherever we are." She leaned in and kissed him.

The dogs sat at their sides.

The only sound was muffled traffic from the square.

"What do you mean—wherever we are?" Josh asked when they came up for air.

"You got that job you interviewed for, didn't you?"

He nodded.

The dark night hid her expression.

"I'm not taking it."

"Did one of the Highpointe jobs come through?" Her tone was hopeful.

"No. But something else came up—just like you said it would." He told her about his conversation with Frank.

"That sounds like the perfect opportunity for you. Congratulations." Sunday dried a tear with her gloved hand. "Now we can both stop looking for jobs."

"You were applying for positions?"

Sunday told him how she'd spent her afternoon. "I want to build a life with you, Josh. Not one apart from you."

"You love being Highpointe's head librarian." Josh blinked hard. "I can't believe you'd give that up. I would never have asked you to leave it."

"I was offering. I don't want to be three hours away from you."

Dan got to his feet and uttered a single "Woof."

"Thank you, boy." Josh laughed. "I wasn't going to forget. Dan's got something for you." He unhooked the box from Dan's collar and flipped it open. "This ring was in my family. You probably can't see it very well in the dark."

Sunday fished her cell phone out of her pocket and engaged the flashlight app. She shone it on the ring and gasped.

"If you don't like it," Josh began.

"Stop," Sunday said. "It. Is. Stunning. I've had a ring like this on my wedding Pinterest board since I was in high school."

"You really like it?"

Sunday nodded emphatically as he removed the ring from its satin pillow and held it out to her.

Sunday whipped off her glove and slipped the ring finger of her left hand through the platinum setting.

She tilted her head to Josh. "It fits. Perfectly. How did you know?"

"I didn't," Josh said. "I guess this was meant to be."

Sunday melted into his arms, and they kissed until the patience of two good dogs wore thin.

The dogs pranced on the way back to the car as if they understood that a new family had been formed.

CHAPTER 47

John's cell phone rang. The caller was "The One." He dropped Roman and Eve's bowls in front of them, and released them from their sit stay. They dove into their suppers while he reached for his phone.

"Sweetheart," he said.

"Hi! I was afraid I was going to voicemail," Maggie said.

"I was in the middle of feeding the dogs."

"Do you want to call me back? I know how insistent they are at dinnertime."

"Nope. They're eating as we speak. How was the first day of the conference?"

"Fine. The sessions are cutting-edge and informative." Maggie toed off her pumps and lay back on the bed, dangling her feet over the side.

"You were nervous about running into Yolanda or Malcolm Yates. Are they there?"

"I haven't seen them. There are over a thousand attendees, so they could be, but I don't think so."

"With the accusations against him, it would take a lot of hutzpah to show up at a group of his peers."

"Or a need to be the center of attention—whether good or bad. Malcolm falls into that category."

"Is anyone talking about them?"

"Not that I've heard."

"That's a relief. Now you can relax and enjoy the rest of your time there."

"That's my plan. I'll go to the dinner in a few minutes. I'm looking forward to hearing the keynote speaker." She rubbed the soles of her feet together in a gentle massage. "How was your day?"

"Fine. The right amount of busy. I'm so glad Sherry's there. I should have hired another veterinarian years ago." He paused, waiting for her response. "You're not going to say you told me so?"

"Evidently I don't have to," Maggie teased. "I'd better force my feet back into these stupid pumps and head to dinner. I just wanted to hear your voice."

"Call me when you return to your room after dinner," he offered.

"That'll be close to ten. You'll be sound asleep. I'll check in again tomorrow about this time."

"Sounds good," John said. "Relax and have fun, now that you know the coast is clear."

Maggie pushed herself off the bed. She exchanged her gold jewelry for pearls and hit a recalcitrant strand of hair with a blast of hairspray, then headed for the dinner.

She didn't know anyone at her assigned table when she sat down. The group was amiable and, by the time the entrée plates were cleared, she'd exchanged business cards with the people seated on either side of her.

Maggie remembered the most recent conference she'd attended—the one where Yolanda had embarrassed Maggie with insinuations about Paul's financial misdeeds. Thank goodness this time was different, Maggie thought.

The servers began bringing in the dessert course. The keynote speaker would soon take the stage.

Maggie excused herself and went to the ladies' room. She took her place at the end of a long line. Two women in front of her were huddled together, whispering and laughing. The tone of their voices and the facial expression of one of the women told Maggie that they were exchanging mean-spirited gossip. She squared her shoulders and ignored them.

One of the women noted Maggie's name tag. "You're her!" she blurted out.

Maggie looked from left to right, hoping the woman was addressing someone else.

"Maggie Martin," the woman said. Now both women had turned to Maggie as the line to the stalls inched along.

Maggie gave a wan smile.

"We were just talking about you. And that bitch, Yolanda Yates." She slurred the epithet.

Maggie took a step back. The last thing she wanted to do

was get into a conversation with one—and probably two—tipsy women.

"She had some nerve dumping on you and your late husband," the other woman said, swaying slightly.

"Yolanda was a stuck-up cow," the woman continued. "Acted like she was better than everyone else at these conferences." Her voice grew louder.

"What goes around comes around," the first woman was practically shouting. "I'll bet her husband is guilty of everything he's charged with."

The people in the front of the line turned to look at the spectacle behind them.

"Me, too. You can't tell me Yolanda didn't know. The wife always knows. It's about time she got what was coming to her."

Maggie was aware of everyone staring at them. A niggling voice at the back of her mind spoke to her.

"You must hate the bitch," the first woman said.

Something inside Maggie snapped. She suspected similar discussions about her and Paul had taken place years ago. Had anyone stood up for Maggie then? She would never know, but she was certain of what she should do now.

"No." She projected her response with steely resolve. "I don't hate Yolanda. I feel compassion for her. I know what it feels like to be betrayed. Support from people you thought you knew—and thought were on your side—evaporates overnight. It's like you're swimming one minute and caught in a rip current the next. But you don't have to be pulled under."

The two women and everyone in line ahead of them looked at Maggie, eyes wide.

"Yolanda says she doesn't know anything about the accusations against her husband. I believe her. Whether they are true or not, her life is hell right now. None of us would trade places with her."

"But she …"

Maggie continued. "If I could talk to her, I'd tell her that I wish her and her family well. That she's strong enough to get through this and that, one day, it'll all be over. Whether or not she and Malcolm stay together, she can weather the storm and be happy again."

The room remained quiet as the women used the facilities and exited.

Maggie was the last one in the room. She lingered, giving herself time to recover from her emotional outburst.

She was applying lipstick and smoothing her hair when the door of the stall at the end of the row opened. Yolanda Yates stepped out.

Their eyes met in the long, rectangular mirror over the sinks.

Yolanda blinked rapidly. "I … you …" She swallowed hard.

Maggie pushed the cap onto her lipstick and shoved it into her purse.

"I'm … so … so very … sorry," Yolanda choked out. She gripped the edge of the sink with both hands, her arms stiff, as she looked into the bowl.

"Believe me, Yolanda. I know how you feel."

"You didn't lash out at an innocent stranger," she said in a rush.

"No." Maggie took a step toward her and put a hand on the other woman's elbow. "But I sure felt like it. Denial, anger, and blaming someone else are all normal."

"You're being kind. I knew that stuff I posted about you and Paul was a lie. I never should have done it."

"You were being human. People make mistakes."

Yolanda nodded. "I've been making a lot of them." Her breath was a shudder. "Like coming here. To this damned convention, where everyone hates me."

Maggie rested her hip against a sink. "Why did you come?"

"Malcolm insisted. He said it would make him look bad if I didn't come."

"Do you care what Malcolm wants? How about taking care of yourself? Subjecting yourself to this isn't good for you."

Yolanda nodded. "I see that, now that I'm here. I can't figure out how to get myself out of the mess I'm in."

Maggie caught Yolanda's gaze and held it. "Get help. Find a good therapist—for yourself. Consult an attorney—again, for yourself, and not for Malcolm or the two of you. You need your own team. They'll help you understand your situation and make solid decisions going forward."

"It's so obvious when you say it like that." Yolanda stood taller.

"It's impossible to throw yourself a lifeline when you're the one drowning." Maggie smiled at Yolanda.

Yolanda smiled back. "Thank you. I'm sorry I was such a … bitch … to you."

"You're forgiven." Maggie squeezed Yolanda's elbow, then released it. "Don't spend any more time thinking about me. That's in the past. Go forward and live a happy life."

Yolanda nodded in solemn agreement.

"And now, I'd better get back to my table, before someone concludes I'm not returning and eats my dessert."

Maggie and Yolanda smiled at each other before Maggie left the room, each of them lightened by the balm of compassion and forgiveness.

THE END

THANK YOU FOR READING

If you enjoyed *Waves of Grace,* I'd be grateful if you wrote a review.

Just a few lines on Amazon or Goodreads would be great. Reviews are the best gift an author can receive. They encourage us when they're good, help us improve our next book when they're not, and help other readers make informed choices when purchasing books. Goodreads reviews help readers find new books. Reviews on Amazon keep the Amazon algorithms humming and are the most helpful aide in selling books! Thank you.

To post a review on Amazon:

1. Go to the product detail page for *Waves of Grace* on Amazon.com.
2. Click "Write a customer review" in the Customer Reviews section.

THANK YOU FOR READING

3. Write your review and click Submit.

In gratitude,
    Barbara Hinske

JUST FOR YOU

Wonder what Maggie was thinking when the book ended? Exclusively for readers who finished *Waves of Grace,* take a look at Maggie's Diary Entry for that day at https://barbarahinske.com/maggies-diary.

ACKNOWLEDGMENTS

I'm blessed with the wisdom and support of many kind and generous people. I want to thank the most supportive and delightful group of champions an author could hope for:

My remarkable husband, Brian Willis, who never fails to steer me

My life coach Mat Boggs for your wisdom and guidance;

My kind and generous legal team, Kenneth Kleinberg, Esq., and Michael McCarthy—thank you for believing in my vision;

The professional "dream team" of my editors Linden Gross, Dione Benson, and proofreader Dana Lee;

Elizabeth Mackey for a beautiful cover.

RECURRING CHARACTERS

<u>Recurring Characters</u>
   ACOSTA
   Grace: older sister to Tommy; David Wheeler's high school sweetheart; plans to attend Highpointe College upon graduation; babysits for the Scanlons
   Iris: mother to Grace and Tommy with husband, Kevin
   Kevin: professor at Highpointe College
   Tommy: became friends with Nicole Nash and David Wheeler while an in-patient at Mercy Hospital
   Alistair: butler at Rosemont for over fifty years, now a friendly ghost who lives in the attic
   John Allen: veterinarian and owner of Westbury Animal Hospital, Maggie Martin's husband, adopted grandfather to baby Julia and twins Sophie and Sarah
   Anita Archer: owner of Archer's Bridal

RECURRING CHARACTERS

Kevin Baxter: member of Highpointe College Board of Trustees

Marc Benson: partner of Alex Scanlon, musician

Nigel Blythe: owner of Blythe Rare Books in London, bought books stolen from Highpointe College Library, poisoned Hazel Harrington, attempted to kill Sunday Sloan and Anthony Plume

Harriet and Larry Burman: owners of Burman Jewelers

Jeff Carson: Widower; former wife, Millie, died 3 years ago; son Jason and daughter-in-law Sharon; grandchildren Tyler and Talia; cares about animal shelter; mother, Alma, uncle, William Olsson

Charlotte: owner of Candy Alley Candy Shop

DELGADO BROTHERS: involved in scheme to embezzle money from the Westbury Town Workers' Pension Fund

Chuck: former Westbury town councilmember; owner of D's Liquor and Convenience Store

Ron: investment advisor and CPA; married to William Wheeler's sister

FITZPATRICK

Laura: owner of Laura's Bakery; mother of one with husband, Pete

Pete: owner of Pete's Bistro, a popular lunch spot for Westbury town councilmembers

Gloria Harper: resident of Fairview Terraces, married to Glenn Vaughn, acts as surrogate grandmother to David Wheeler

Hazel Harrington: deceased rare-book librarian at Highpointe College, poisoned by Nigel Blythe

RECURRING CHARACTERS

Robert Harris: rare-book librarian at Cambridge University, friend to Sunday Sloan

Frank Haynes: repentant crony of the Delgados, Westbury town councilmember, owner of Haynes Enterprises (holding company of fast food restaurants), founder and principal funder of Forever Friends dog rescue, grandson of Hector Martin, married to Loretta Nash, father of twins Bonnie and Branson

HOLMES

George: emcee of the annual Easter Carnival, father of three with wife, Tonya

Tonya: Westbury town councilmember; close friend of Maggie Martin

Russell Isaac: Westbury town councilmember, inherited auto parts business, former acting mayor of Westbury, involved in the scheme to embezzle money with the Delgado brothers

Lyla Kershaw: works in accounting department at Highpointe College Library; close friend of Sunday Sloan; birth mother of Josh Newlon

Tim Knudsen: realtor, Westbury town councilmember, married to Nancy, grandfather to Zack

Ian Lawry: former president of Highpointe College

Ingrid: Haynes family nanny, former pediatric ICU nurse

Juan: veterinary technician at Westbury Animal Hospital

MARTIN

Amy: Maggie Martin's daughter-in-law; mother to twins, Sophie and Sarah, with husband, Mike Martin

Hector and Silas: deceased town patriarchs; Silas (Hector's father) amassed a fortune from the local sawmill, real estate, and other ventures and built the Rosemont estate; Hector donated his rare book collection to Highpointe College and left his estate to his living heirs—grandnephew, Paul Martin, and grandson, Frank Haynes (Frank's father was Hector's illegitimate son)

Maggie: current owner of Rosemont and president of Highpointe College; widow of Paul Martin; former forensic accountant and mayor of Westbury; married to John Allen; mother to Mike Martin and Susan (Martin) Scanlon; grandmother to Julia Scanlon and twins, Sophie and Sarah Martin

Mike: Maggie Martin's adult son, lives in California with wife, Amy, and twin daughters, Sophie and Sarah

Paul: Maggie Martin's first husband, deceased; embezzled funds while president of Windsor College; father of Susan (Martin) Scanlon and Mike Martin; had an affair with Loretta Nash and fathered Nicole Nash

Sophie and Sarah: twin daughters of Amy and Mike Martin; close friends of Marissa Nash; Maggie Martin's granddaughter

Mary: single mother who is the administrative assistant at Haynes Enterprises

Gordon Mortimer: antiques dealer and appraiser

NASH

Loretta: current financial analyst at Haynes Enterprises; married to Frank Haynes; mother to Marissa, Sean, and Nicole, with baby number four on the way; former mistress of Paul Martin

Marissa, Nicole, Sean: Loretta's children, adopted by stepfather, Frank Haynes; Marissa (oldest) babysits for the Scanlons and is friends with Maggie Martin's twin granddaughters; Nicole (youngest) received a kidney from Susan Scanlon after it was discovered that they had the same father, Paul Martin; Sean works as David Wheeler's apprentice at Forever Friends and the animal hospital

Bonnie and Branson: Frank and Loretta's twins

Josh Newlon: Maggie Martin's administrative assistant; Lyla Kershaw's birth son; Sunday Sloan's boyfriend

PARKER

Sherry and Neil: Sherry is the new veterinarian at Westbury Animal Hospital and her husband, Neil, is a graduate of The Warton School

Anthony Plume: professor and dean of English Literature at Highpointe College; stole rare books from the college library and sold them to Nigel Blythe

Jack Rodriguez: David Wheeler's landlord in California

SCANLON

Aaron: orthopedic surgeon; married to Maggie's daughter, Susan; father to baby Julia; brother to Alex

Alex: attorney who succeeds Maggie Martin as mayor of Westbury; partner of Marc Benson

Julia: infant daughter of Susan and Aaron Scanlon; Maggie Martin's granddaughter

Susan (*née Martin*): Maggie Martin's adult daughter; attorney works at brother-in-law Alex's firm; helped Josh Newlon find his birth mother; nearly died donating kidney to stepsister, Nicole Nash

Sunday Sloan: rare-book librarian at Highpointe College; friend of Lyla Kershaw; Josh Newlon's girlfriend

Forest Smith: attorney at Stetson & Graham; assigned to assist Alex Scanlon; died in a suspicious fall off a bridge

Bill Stetson: partner at Stetson & Graham, Westbury's outside law firm

Chief Andrew (Andy) Thomas: Westbury's chief of police

Joan and Sam Torres: wife and husband; Maggie Martin's close friends, who befriended her on her first day in Westbury; Joan works as a police dispatcher, Sam as a handyman

Lyndon Upton: professor of finance at University of Chicago, former colleague of Maggie Martin's; volunteered to help with Westbury's embezzlement case

Glenn Vaughn: resident of Fairview Terraces; married to Gloria Harper; acts as surrogate grandfather to David Wheeler

WHEELER

David: works with therapy dogs; helps at Forever Friends and Westbury Animal Hospital; son of William and Jackie Wheeler; Grace Acosta's boyfriend

Jackie: wife of disgraced former mayor William Wheeler; mother to David

William: former mayor of Westbury convicted for fraud and embezzlement; committed suicide in prison; father to David and husband to Jackie

Yolanda and Malcolm Yates: Malcolm is president of a

college and was a colleague of Paul Martin. Yolanda is his wife.

Judy Young: business-savvy owner of Celebrations Gift Shop and town gossip; close friend of Maggie Martin; maiden name Jorgenson

RECURRING PETS

Pets

Blossom, Buttercup, and Bubbles—Maggie and John's kittens, named after PowerPuff Girls

Cara—small female German Shepherd adopted by Josh Newlon. Black with a caramel-colored face

Cooper—Susan and Aaron Scanlon's dog, a gift from David Wheeler. A young Golden Retriever who is calm and gentle with baby Julia

Daisy—Nash children's dog, an Aussie/cattle dog mix female

Dan—Josh Newlon's dog, huge black lab, has calming effect on baby Julia

Dodger—David Wheeler's dog, mid-sized mutt with one eye. Therapy dog

Dory—Jack Rodriguez's Westie

Eve—shows up at Rosemont on Maggie's first night, stray, small female terrier mix

Magellan—Tommy Acosta's cat

Namor—David Wheeler's cat whose name is Roman spelled backward, gray with 4 white paws

Roman—John Allen's dog, gentle Golden Retriever

Rusty—Sam and Joan Torres's dog

Sally—Frank Haynes' dog, overweight border collie mix

Snowball—Nash children's dog, a terrier/schnauzer mix male

Sparky—Tim Knudsen's grandson's dog/medium-sized crossbreed with curly brown and white coat

ABOUT THE AUTHOR

USA Today Bestselling and Amazon All Star Author BARBARA HINSKE is an attorney and novelist. She loves to read and write women's fiction, mystery/thriller/suspense, and sweet Christmas stories. She's authored the Guiding Emily series, the mystery thriller collection "Who's There?", the Paws & Pastries series, three of the novellas in The Wishing Tree series, and the beloved Rosemont series. Her novella *The Christmas Club* and novel *Guiding Emily* have both been adapted for Hallmark Channel.

ENJOY THIS EXCERPT FROM GUIDING EMILY

Prologue

Emily. The woman who would become everything to me. The person I would eat every meal with and lie down next to every night—for the rest of my days.

She was just ahead; behind that door at the far end of the long hall. I glanced over my shoulder. Mark kept pace, slightly behind me. I could feel his excitement. It matched my own.

Everyone said Emily and I would be perfect for each other. I'd overheard them talking when they thought I was asleep. I spend a lot of time with my eyes closed, but I don't sleep much. They didn't know that.

"A magical match," they'd all agreed.

I lifted my eyes to Mark, and he nodded his encouragement. I gave a brief shake of my head. Only four more doorways between Emily and me.

I picked up my pace. A cylindrical orange object on the carpet in the third doorway from the end caught my eye. *Is that a Cheeto? A Crunchy Cheeto? I love Crunchy Cheetos.*

I tore my eyes away.

This was no time to get distracted.

We sped across the remaining distance to the doorway at the end of the hall. The door that separated me from my destiny.

I froze and waited while Mark knocked.

I heard Emily's voice—the sound I would come to love above all others—say, "Come in."

What was that in her voice? Eagerness—anxiety—maybe even a touch of fear? I'd take care of all of that right away.

The door swung open and Mark stepped back. He pointed to Emily.

I'd seen her before. Emily Main was a beautiful young woman in her late twenties. Auburn hair cascaded around her shoulders and shone like a new penny. With my jet-black coloring, we'd make a striking couple.

"Go on," Mark said.

I abandoned all my training—all sense of decorum—and raced to her.

Emily reached for me and flung her arms around my neck.

I placed my nose against her throat, and she tumbled out of her chair onto her knees.

I swept my tongue over her cheek, tasting the saltiness of her tears.

"Oh … Garth." My name on her lips came out in a hoarse whisper.

I wagged my tail so hard that we both lay back on the floor. "Good boy, Garth!"

She rubbed the ridge of my skull behind my ears in a way that would become one of my favorite things in the whole wide world.

Next to food.

Especially Crunchy Cheetos.

Mark and the other trainers were right—we were made for each other. I was the perfect guide dog for Emily Main.

Chapter 1

"Weren't you supposed to leave for the airport half an hour ago?" Michael Ward asked his boss, whose fingers were typing furiously on her keyboard. "You're still planning to get married, aren't you?"

Emily Main's head bobbed behind the computer, her eyes fixed to the screen.

"I can't believe you put off a departure to Fiji to help us launch this new program. Your wedding's in two days."

"We've been working on this for almost a year. I wasn't about to leave when we're this close. I just need to finish this last email." She hunched forward and peered at the computer screen.

"There," she said, pushing her office chair back as the email *whooshed* from her inbox. "Done."

She looked up at Michael, blinking. It was probably the

ENJOY THIS EXCERPT FROM GUIDING EMILY

first time she had looked at anything besides a computer screen in hours. "I brought my suitcase so I could go to the airport straight from the office. I don't have to stop at home."

Michael raised his eyebrows at her. "That's all you've got? A carry-on and a satchel for a week—a week that includes your wedding? My wife packs more than that for a three-day weekend."

"My wedding dress is a classic sheath and the rest is bathing suits and shorts."

"I would have thought Connor Harrington the third would have wanted an elaborate wedding—one fit for the society pages."

"Our wedding is going to be very elegant—think JFK Junior and Carolyn," Emily said, flinging her purse over her shoulder and reaching for the retractable handle of her suitcase.

Michael stepped in front of her. "I've got this," he said. "I'll walk you to the street. I'd like to congratulate Connor on snagging our office hero."

Emily hesitated.

"He is picking you up, isn't he? You're flying there together?"

"He went out over the weekend. He wanted to do some diving with his best man ... sort of a bachelor party reprise. I was traveling with my mom and maid of honor, but they flew out yesterday as planned. The company paid to change my ticket, but it would have cost almost five hundred dollars for Mom and Gina to change theirs. It wasn't worth it."

"But you don't like to fly." He peered into Emily's face.

"Did you talk to Connor about that before you decided to stay an extra day? You have told him about your fear of flying, haven't you?"

Emily shrugged. "I've mentioned it, sure, but I haven't made a big deal out of it."

"So what did he say?"

"He suggested that I get a prescription for Xanax and sleep the whole way out there."

"Really? That's what he said?"

"He's a Brit, for heaven's sake. 'Stiff upper lip' and all that. He's not the sort of guy to coddle anyone—and I'm not a needy type of gal. You know that."

Michael cocked his head to one side. "Do you have to change planes?"

Emily nodded.

"You don't want to be knocked out for that."

"I'll be fine." Emily threw her shoulders back. "You don't need to worry about me."

"I know—I'm sorry. It's just that I wouldn't let my wife make the trip alone if she felt like you do about flying."

"I fly alone all the time, and nothing's ever happened to me. There's no reason this time should be any different."

Michael lifted his hands, palms facing her, and shrugged. "Okay, but I think he could have at least offered to pay to change your mom's flight or something."

"I'll be perfectly fine." Emily walked past him into the hallway. "I promised Dhruv that I'd say goodbye before I leave."

"He's going to miss you. You're the one person here that really connects with him."

Michael watched her shoulders sag slightly.

"Hey," he said, rolling the carry-on to a halt beside her in the hall. "I'm sorry. I didn't mean to worry you. The whole team is going to step into your shoes while you're gone. We've talked about it."

"Of course you will. I shouldn't worry about him. I've got the best team in San Francisco. Scratch that. On the entire West Coast." Emily gave him a teary smile and punched him playfully on the shoulder. "I know you'll take care of everything while I'm away, Michael—including helping Dhruv stay connected with the team."

"Good!" Michael continued down the hallway. "I don't want you to give this place a second thought while you're gone. If anyone deserves a vacation—and a gorgeous beach wedding—it's you, Em. But don't get too comfortable." Michael turned and smiled at her. "We do need you to come back. We'd be lost without you here."

Emily laughed and pushed him toward the elevator. "Why don't you go push that button, you wonderful suck-up. It'll take ages to get an elevator this time of the morning. I'll stick my head into Dhruv's cubicle and be right back."

***

Emily found Dhruv, as usual, leaning into the bank of computer monitors, intently focused on the complex strings of code in front of him. She cleared her throat.

When Dhruv didn't move, she tapped him lightly on the shoulder.

Dhruv sat back quickly and spun around. A smile spread across his face when he saw her.

"I wanted to say goodbye before I go."

Dhruv nodded. "Goodbye."

"I'll see you a week from Monday."

"I know. You're getting married in two days, then you have your honeymoon for a week, then you come back to work," he recited.

"That's right. You remembered."

"I remember things."

"Yes, you do. That's one reason you're so very good at programming," she said.

"I know."

"Okay ... well ... have a good week. You can go to Michael if you have ... if you need anything."

"I know."

Emily regarded the shy, socially awkward middle-aged man who was, by far, the most proficient member of her extremely talented team of programmers. "Bye."

Dhruv nodded.

Emily stepped away.

Dhruv leapt out of his chair and called after her. "Have a happy wedding."

Emily swung around and gave him a thumbs-up then turned back toward the elevators where Michael was waiting.

From *Guiding Emily*

ALSO BY BARBARA HINSKE

Available at Amazon in Print, Audio, and for Kindle

The Rosemont Series

Coming to Rosemont

Weaving the Strands

Uncovering Secrets

Drawing Close

Bringing Them Home

Shelving Doubts

Restoring What Was Lost

No Matter How Far

When Dreams There Be

Waves of Grace

Novellas

The Night Train

The Christmas Club (adapted for The Hallmark Channel, 2019)

Paws & Pastries

Sweets & Treats

Snowflakes, Cupcakes & Kittens

Workout Wishes & Valentine Kisses

Wishes of Home

Wishful Tails

Back in the Pack

Novels in the Guiding Emily Series

Guiding Emily (adapted for The Hallmark Channel, 2023)

The Unexpected Path

Over Every Hurdle

Down the Aisle

From the Heart

Novels in the "Who's There?!" Collection

Deadly Parcel

Final Circuit

CONNECT WITH BARBARA HINSKE ONLINE

Sign up for her newsletter at **BarbaraHinske.com**
    Goodreads.com/BarbaraHinske
    Facebook.com/BHinske
    Instagram/barbarahinskeauthor
    TikTok.com/BarbaraHinske
    Pinterest.com/BarbaraHinske
    X.com/BarbaraHinske
    Search for **Barbara Hinske on YouTube**
    <u>bhinske@gmail.com</u>

Printed in Great Britain
by Amazon

48602425R00189